CHASING THE BULLET

"How come you were trying to capture that blue stallion?" asked Dixie.

"Because he's worth a thousand dollars' reward."

Ruff wasn't sure that he'd heard correctly. "Did you say 'a thousand dollars'?"

"I did! That renegade stallion is faster than a bullet, that's how he got his name. Two years ago Blue Bullet broke free and he's been outwitting everyone who's tried to put a lasso on him since."

"If 'everyone' is as stupid as you and Milt," Dixie commented, "being outwitted by a horse doesn't surprise me."

"Me neither." Ruff bristled. "What would have happened if your fifty-caliber ball had broken that stallion's neck?"

There was a long silence and then Pete muttered, "You got to remember, there are no guarantees in life, mister. Not for a man or a horse."

Ruff's fist doubled up and he almost punched the callous fool, helpless or not. "I got no use for your kind," he said, voice ragged with outrage. "Is there a sheriff in Rum River?"

"You bet, and when he sees what you did to Milt's leg, I'll have the last laugh on both of you! You'll be lucky if you don't hang, and I hope you by-gawd do!"

THE HORSEMEN

BLUE BULLET

GARY McCARTHY

DIAMOND BOOKS, NEW YORK

This book is a Diamond original
edition, and has never been
previously published.

BLUE BULLET

A Diamond Book / published by arrangement with
the author

PRINTING HISTORY
Diamond edition / September 1993

ISBN: 1-55773-944-7

Diamond Books are published by The Berkley Publishing
Group, 200 Madison Avenue, New York, New York 10016.
DIAMOND and the "D" design are trademarks
belonging to Charter Communications, Inc.

PRINTED IN THE UNITED STATES OF AMERICA

10 9 8 7 6 5 4 3 2 1

To the Corral #5
River Rats
Wherever They May Yet Ride

ONE

Rufus "Ruff" Ballou squinted his eyes against the rising sun and gazed out across an ocean of majestic mountain ranges. As far as he could see, the snow-capped Sangre de Cristos lifted like towering cathedrals of stone. Under his long legs, his four-year-old Thoroughbred stallion, High Fire, shifted impatiently. Maybe it, too, was remembering the sweet bluegrass of their Tennessee home and felt awed by this great western mountain range.

"Tough country," Ruff said, pale blue eyes taking in the distant Rio Grande from the vantage of an immense granite ridge. "Pretty, in its own way, though. Don't you think?"

Beside him, Dixie Ballou, scoffed. She was fifteen years old, and at an age where nothing impressed her, not even the unspoiled splendor of the American West. "This country isn't fit for anything but growing rattlesnakes and scorpions. I still don't understand why we didn't build our new horse ranch around Austin, Texas."

"You know why," Ruff told his fifteen-year-old sister. "The farther west we ride, the better it'll be for our health."

Ruff didn't need to say any more, and Dixie looked away to hide her bitterness. Neither one of them could ever forget how the Civil War and the need for swift horses had driven the Ballous westward in order to preserve the last two great foundation sires of their famed Thoroughbred bloodline. But in the process of fleeing before the advancing army of the North, there'd been a succession of devastating losses. Their father had been shot down by their own Confederate soldiers while attempting to defend his last few stallions from

1

becoming cannon fodder and, in so doing, had branded the Ballous as traitors to the South. And this in spite of the fact that Ruff's two eldest brothers had fallen as heroes on the blood-drenched battlefields of Shiloh and Bull Run. And finally, there was the story of Ruff's third brother, the hot-headed romantic, Houston, who now languished in some Federal hellhole prison near Washington. Charged as a Confederate spy, he might already have been executed by the Union.

Ruff lived with the burden of knowing that he was the last free man of his once illustrious Southern family. The one responsible not only for Dixie, but for his father's life's work—the raising of the finest racehorses in America. Before the Civil War, the name Ballou had stood for respect, but that respect was now sullied and coupled with the epitaph *traitor*. It was a name with a bounty attached to it for the killing of a foolish and ruthlessly ambitious Confederate officer.

"Ruff? How far do we have to run to escape our past?" Dixie asked, her expression forlorn because she had left her heart back at their Wildwood Farm in the gentle bluegrass hills of Tennessee. "We can't run forever."

"And the war can't last many more years," Ruff said. "But if it does, we'll breed the finest horses in the world and supply them to the Confederacy. But we'll do it our way, and not theirs. And we'll find a way to clear our family name."

Dixie dismounted and checked her cinch. She was, like her brothers, tall for her age, with dark hair and eyes and a still-boyish figure that she was not pleased about losing. Dixie liked to ride fast horses and she was flirting with cuss words. "Ruff, do you have any idea where the hell we are?"

He studied the distant river and the towering ramparts of mountains that lifted and folded as far as the eye could carry. "These are the Sangre de Cristo Mountains, so we must be well into the New Mexico Territory."

"I know that much!"

Ruff dismounted and checked his own cinch. He was six feet four and as whippishly lean as his Thoroughbred stallion. Dark haired and black eyed thanks to the Cherokee blood on his mother's side, Ruff looked much older than his nineteen years. Maybe it was because of his missing earlobe, a memento of his own brush with death during the war, or perhaps it was because of his weighty responsibilities coupled with the loss of his father and brothers. What kept him going was Dixie and these last four Thoroughbred horses. They were his Tennessee legacy. His only hope for a better tomorrow.

Ruff stroked High Fire's muscular neck and then walked back and ran his hand down the legs of the two Thoroughbred brood mares that constituted the last of their once-great stable of Southern racehorses. Satisfied that the mares were holding up well, Ruff remounted High Fire.

"Santa Fe must be only a few miles up the Rio Grande. All we got to do is to follow 'er, Dixie. Might be we can reach Santa Fe by nightfall."

"Not very damned likely," Dixie groused. "Why, I don't see a living thing down there."

"You would if you looked hard enough," Ruff said with just a hint of amusement.

Dixie shot a questioning glance at Ruff and tugged her own hat down low over her eyes. She could not abide her brother knowing or seeing anything that she could not. Inch by careful inch, Dixie scanned the vast sea of forest and rock. Minutes passed and her irritation mounted. "There's nothing down there!"

"Sure, there is! Lookee yonder along that first ridge of mountains. Up where that flashing trickle of water shoots off that cliff. See that flashy blue stallion and his band of mustang mares? He's sure got his eye on us."

Dixie saw them and was irritated at herself because the mustangs were less than a mile away while she'd been looking at the soaring distances beyond. "I was searching for horsemen."

"Well, you said there was nary a living thing, and that's a pretty fair-sized band of wild horses. That blue stallion has a sharp eye for danger. See how wary he acts."

The blue stallion was upset. Dixie could see him prancing back and forth, throwing his head and then stopping to rear up on his hind legs. And across the crystal-clear void that separated humans from the twenty or so mustangs, Dixie suddenly heard the blue's trumpeting challenge. High Fire and then old High Man bugled a throaty reply. The Ballou mares lifted their heads expectantly and whinnied.

"My, my," Dixie said, "that blue stallion is a fine piece of horseflesh unless my eyes are failing."

"They're not failing at all," Ruff said, admiring the blue and the quality of his mustang mares. "He's a beauty and I'll wager he owns some Thoroughbred blood."

"You think so?"

"Sure! A horse that big and tall—and with that kind of action and grace—has to be the product of careful breeding and selection. My guess is that he has probably escaped some wealthy horse breeder and adapted to this high mountain country. It's obvious that he's laid claim to a pretty fine band of mares. Not a scrub among them."

Dixie didn't argue. When it came to horses, the only man who understood and could judge them better than Ruff had been their late father, Justin. Ruff had inherited all Justin's equine instincts and knowledge and, in Dixie's admittedly biased opinion, was the finest horseman alive.

"That stallion and his high-quality mares would be worth some pretty good money," Ruff mused.

"Oh no," Dixie warned, seeing a familiar gleam of interest and excitement in her brother's eyes. "We'd cripple our Thoroughbreds if we were to go chasing after that band. They're probably used to flying over these mountain rocks and ridges like mountain goats. If we're going to do any running in New Mexico, I insist that it be on a flat dirt racing track."

"You're probably right," Ruff conceded. "It's just that we're pretty near broke, Dixie. One way or another, we've got to figure out some way to earn spending cash. These horses could use grain and we're about out of coffee, sugar, salt, and staples. Pretty low on ammunition, too."

"Maybe we can find work in Santa Fe."

"Maybe." Ruff touched spurs to High Fire's flanks and the young sorrel stallion eagerly stepped ahead, perhaps hoping that he'd be allowed to challenge the blue mustang for his mares.

"Not a chance," Ruff told his excited horse. "That big stud down yonder would eat you up and spit you out for breakfast. He's your height and heavier muscled."

In reply, High Fire whinnied another challenge to show that he was not the least bit intimidated. Ruff chuckled and twisted around in his saddle to see that even old High Man, their foundation sire, was showing off, dancing and shaking his head.

Dixie did not look amused.

Ruff was just about to suggest that they ride another hour or two before they stopped and ate cold biscuits for breakfast when suddenly, two booming rifle shots crashed and rolled like clapping thunder between the mountain peaks. Ruff twisted around in his saddle in time to see a pair of men with buffalo rifles emerge from the rocks about a half mile away. They shouted at the retreating band of mustangs who, except for one downed mare, now escaped into the forest.

"They shot one!" Dixie cried in anger and outrage. "A mare is down!"

Ruff Ballou was normally easygoing except when it came to the mistreatment of animals, most particularly horses, though he'd been known to fight over the cruel abuse of dogs, mules, and even cats. And the mare was dying; that much was obvious from the way she thrashed helplessly against the earth, barely able to raise her head.

"Here!" Ruff shouted, tossing the mares' lead ropes to Dixie.

"Ruff, wait for me! There's two of them!"

"Stay out of this!" Ruff shouted as he sent High Fire skidding down the mountainside in a cloud of dust and sliding shale.

The two mustang killers saw Ruff coming and they must have been able to read his murderous expression because they immediately knelt and started trying to reload their powerful single-shot buffalo rifles. Dixie held her breath and watched with amazement as her brother drove High Fire forward. Somehow, horse and rider reached the flats below. Ruff and his tall Thoroughbred streaked across the land, bearing down on the two hunters like a runaway train. Just as the first hunter began to lift his reloaded weapon, High Fire's shoulder knocked him flying like a broken rag doll.

The second man did finish reloading and he even managed to lift his rifle but before he could take aim, Ruff launched himself from his saddle. When he slammed into the rifleman, they both tumbled and rolled, gouging and punching. It was Ruff's misfortune to butt up against a rock underneath his heavier opponent. The man had a dirty black beard and deep-set, pitiless eyes.

Spittle sprayed Ruff's face as the man cried, "Goddammit, I'll smash your face in!"

And he would have if Ruff had not thrown his head

sideways so that the man's fist broke against the unforgiving earth.

"Owwww!"

Ruff kicked upward with his long, horseman's legs and wrapped them around the bearded man's neck. With a powerful downward contraction, he yanked his opponent over backward. In an instant, he was on his feet and leaping on the man, fists a blur of knuckled fury. Three times Ruff sledged the horse killer in the face until the man's eyes rolled upward and his body went limp.

Ruff grabbed the man's beard in his hands and slammed his head down against the rocky ground twice out of sheer pent-up rage.

"Ruff, look out!" Dixie called, urging High Man and their mares down the mountainside as fast as she could without them losing their footing to somersault down the treacherous slope.

Ruff whirled and saw the first man attacking with a bowie knife. He was huge and wore a crazed expression. Ruff did the only thing that any reasonable person would do in his precarious circumstances: he coolly drew his Army Colt.

"Halt or I'll shoot!"

But the man must have been dazed from being struck by High Fire because he didn't seem to comprehend. He just kept coming, so Ruff aimed low and fired.

The attacker howled and lurched sideways before collapsing in a pile. Blood poured from a gaping bullet hole in his upper leg. But when Ruff came over to help, the man cursed and took a nasty swipe at him with the bowie knife. If Ruff hadn't been blessed with the reflexes of a cougar, he'd have been hamstrung. Instead, he jumped back and then kicked. The toe of his boot connected solidly at the point of the wounded man's chin. It could easily have broken his thick neck, but instead put the fool to sleep.

Ruff hurried over to the fallen mare. She was a bay, with two stockings and a pretty blaze—a fine-looking horse. When Ruff laid his hand on her muzzle, the mare's glazing eyes pleaded for mercy. Ruff studied the bright red blood that was oozing from her chest.

"They shot you through the lungs," Ruff whispered, his voice choking with anger. "No reason for either of 'em to do such an awful thing to such a pretty girl as yourself. No damned reason at all!"

Ruff's gun was still clenched in his fist. With a sad shake of his head, he placed his free hand over the mare's glazing eye and then he rested the muzzle of his Colt against her forehead. The blast of his Army Colt filled the air and singed the hair around the bullet hole. But the mare sighed with relief and went limp in death.

Dixie arrived to place a hand on Ruff's shoulder before turning to study the unconscious horse killers. "Why?"

"I don't know," he said between teeth locked in anger. "Some men just like to shoot things and maybe that's what happened here. Or they might have been trying to kill that blue stallion to keep him from stealing other mares. I just don't know."

"That fella you shot in the thigh could bleed to death if we don't do something."

Ruff jammed his six-gun back into his holster. "If you want to apply a tourniquet, go ahead. Me, I don't care if he survives or not."

"I don't, either. But I don't want a New Mexico lawman on our backtrail for killing one man and almost beating another's brains out."

Ruff wasn't listening. He stroked the dead mare's neck and thought, What a waste of fine horseflesh! What in blazes did men such as these have in their minds when they opened fire? It wasn't as if they were starving for horse meat.

No sir! It was, as near as Ruff could tell, either on account of blood lust or meanness. It was sad to realize that a few ornery sonsabitches in this world just liked to shoot things so that they could watch them die.

"Here," Dixie said, handing Ruff High Fire's reins and the lead ropes to the mares. "I'll see what I can do for the one that you shot in the leg."

"Maybe I'll have to saw it clean off at the knee with that big bowie knife he was fixin' to use on me."

Ruff tied the Ballou Thoroughbreds in a stand of pines and returned to the unconscious man whose head he'd bounced up and down. He disarmed and rolled him over to examine the back of his skull for any permanent damage. There didn't seem to be any.

"Ruff, I could use some help here!"

Ruff heard the note of desperation in his sister's voice and it jolted him out of his all-consuming anger. Dixie was right, they had to at least try to stop the bleeding and save the man's worthless life if for no other reason than to avoid a run-in with the law.

"It's bad," Dixie said, her voice tight with worry. "Your bullet shattered the leg bone. I'm afraid that it might also have severed an artery."

She looked up for an instant. "He may die, Ruff! We've got to stop this bleeding and get the man to a doctor!"

"Here," Ruff said, tearing his own neckerchief away from his neck and using it as a tourniquet just above the wound. The bleeding didn't stop completely, but almost. "Dixie, just cinch your bandanna right down over the top of the bullet hole and I think we'll manage to get this bleeding stopped."

Dixie did as her brother instructed, but her bandanna soon became saturated with blood. "If he dies, we could be in deep trouble, Ruff."

"He got exactly what he deserved," Ruff said. "Not only did he shoot the mare, but he also tried to gut me with his bowie knife. I ordered the fool to throw down his knife and stop, but he kept coming. I shot him in self-defense."

"Yeah, I know that, but this whole thing could still cause us a peck of trouble!"

Ruff came to his feet. Dixie was often sharp tongued and a trial, but she was also smart and sensible. "Okay," Ruff said, "we'll hunt up a doctor. But first, I'll go up into those rocks to see if they have horses of their own, though I doubt it because that would have prevented them from getting in so close to the mustangs."

Dixie opened her mouth to say something, then seemed to think better of it and changed her mind. "Let's hurry," she finally said. "Dammit! I sure wish none of this happened. We've both already seen more than a lifetime of killing. It seems to follow our family like a curse."

"Yeah, it does," Ruff sadly admitted. "Maybe I lost my head up there on the ridge when I heard those rifles and saw the mare drop. Maybe I should have just stayed out of this trouble."

"No," Dixie said quietly. "Neither of us could have let it pass and then looked ourselves in the mirror. It wasn't your fault and I'm proud of you, Ruff."

Dixie expelled a ragged breath and her face was as pale and bleak as the face of winter. "It's just that trouble haunts us wherever we go, Ruff. And one of these days . . ."

Dixie struggled but couldn't find the words to express her frustration and worry. But Ruff knew what she meant and it filled him with desolation. He'd never considered himself to be a superstitious man, but Ruff couldn't help but think that this horse-killing affair was a bad omen foreshadowing what they might expect in New Mexico.

TWO

Following the Rio Grande north was simple enough, and when Ruff and company passed through a divide and beheld a ranching community nestled in the center of an immense valley, the view was as pleasing as anything he'd yet seen west of the the Pecos River. Even at a distance, the community gave every indication of being both prosperous and permanent, two attributes generally in short supply on the American frontier.

What made the valley itself so spectacular was its deep grass fed by not only the Rio Grande, but also by a rum-colored river that flowed down from the Sangre de Cristos. This river meandered like a lazy stream through the valley, finally joining the Rio Grande where the pretty town was nestled. A New England–style church with a tall alabaster steeple spired upward to tickle the snow-capped mountains beyond.

"I don't know what this place is called," Ruff said. "It's pretty but too small for Santa Fe."

"We can't say that for sure," Dixie argued. "Maybe Santa Fe isn't as big as its reputation."

"This is a ranching community," Ruff informed his sister. "I've heard descriptions of Santa Fe and they don't fit this town. For example, I'm told that Santa Fe has a lot of adobe haciendas with red tile roofs. No, this is definitely not Santa Fe."

"Goddamn you!" the man with the broken skull whined. "This is Rum River! And when we get into town, I'll have you both arrested and sent to the territorial prison!"

11

"Not very damned likely," Dixie snapped. "If there's a sheriff here, we're the ones who will press charges."

"For what!"

"Shooting a horse."

"It was just a goddamn mustang! There's a bounty on 'em in these parts, you idiots!"

Ruff glanced at his sister. "Did you hear what he called us?"

"Yes, and I believe the man needs a lesson in manners."

Ruff walked back to the man tied across the back of a Ballou mare.

"What the hell are you gonna do!"

"What's your name?"

"Pete!" The man gulped. "What are you fixin' to do to me!" Ruff flexed his fingers, then made a fist. "Why, Pete, I'm going to see if I can break your jaw with a single punch."

The man's eyes bulged with fear. Being trussed hand and foot and draped across the back of a horse, he was helpless. "Please, don't hit me!"

Ruff stopped flexing his fingers. His eyebrows knitted and he studied the man as if he were a bug that needed squashing under his thumb. "You apologize?"

"I do!" Pete shook his head and dripped sweat. "I didn't mean to insult you. It's just that you don't know what the hell you're doing! Milt and I were within our rights to shoot that mare even if we did kill the wrong mustang."

"Exactly what horse were you aiming for?

"Blue Bullet, of course!"

"Blue Bullet?" Ruff scratched the stubble at his jaw. "That's the stallion's name?"

"That's right."

"Why were you boys trying to kill him?"

"We wasn't trying to kill him. Not exactly. What we was

trying to do was to crease the back of his neck. You do it just right and you'll stun a horse so's you can blindfold and hobble him before he comes around. It's been a time or two."

Ruff looked to Dixie and he could see that she was also appalled. Ruff shook his head. "A bullet creasing a horse's spine might stun him, but I'll bet nine times out of ten you either shoot low and kill the horse, or shoot high and miss."

"We both shot high," Pete confessed. "Milt shot that bay mare, not me. I missed everything."

"No matter," Dixie said sternly. "You both deserve what you got."

"That's right," Ruff said. "And Milt was coming at me with his bowie knife. I expect you'd have shot me if you could have reloaded faster."

The man's silence confirmed Ruff's assessment. After a minute, curiosity drove Dixie to ask, "How come you and Milt were trying to capture that blue stallion?"

"Because he's worth a thousand dollars' reward."

Ruff wasn't sure that he'd heard correctly. "Did you say 'a thousand dollars'?"

"I did! That renegade stallion is faster than a bullet, that's how he got his name."

"He looks fast," Ruff admitted. "But a thousand dollars? Pete, I find that hard to believe since you can buy most any quality racehorse in Tennessee or Kentucky for a whole lot less money."

"Maybe so," the man said, "but Mr. Jack Grimm doesn't want just any old racehorse. He wants Blue Bullet back again. He had that blue devil shipped over on a boat from England. Two years ago, the stallion broke free and he's been outwitting everyone who's tried to put a lasso on him since."

"If 'everyone' is as stupid as you and Milt," Dixie commented, "being outwitted by a horse doesn't surprise me."

"Me neither." Ruff bristled. "And I still can't believe that anyone would be dumb enough to try and crease a horse's neck. What would have happened if your fifty-caliber ball had broken that stallion's neck?"

There was a long silence and then Pete muttered, "You got to remember, there are no guarantees in life, mister. Not for a man or a horse."

Ruff's fist doubled up and he almost punched the callous fool, helpless or not. "I got no use for your kind," he said, voice ragged with outrage. "Is there a sheriff in Rum River?"

"You bet, and when he sees what you did to Milt's leg, I'll have the last laugh on both of you! You'll be lucky if you don't hang, and I hope you by-gawd do!"

Before he lost his temper, Ruff touched spurs to the flanks of his horse and Dixie was right beside him.

"Mister!" Pete cried out in desperation. "I didn't mean what I just said about you hangin'. Please come back and untie me! My poor head is about to explode like a Mexican firecracker. I'm going to die if I can't sit up straight."

"I don't think that would be a good idea," Dixie cautioned.

Ruff agreed. "We're almost to town. Let's just hope that there's a doctor or at least a tooth puller who can bind up that leg. Is it still bleeding?"

Dixie looked back. Milt remained unconscious but he was gray faced. "I think the bleeding has stopped but he's in real desperate shape."

"We're almost there," Ruff said, pushing High Fire into a trot.

Dixie's was riding High Fire's daddy, the great High Man. And even though their old foundation sire was eighteen years old, he still had a lot of spunk and speed. High

Man wanted to race into the town and he began to dance. Behind him, the mares were forced to trot in order to keep up.

"Stop!" the bearded man howled. "Oh, please! You're pounding the life out of me!"

Ruff swiveled around in his saddle and he had to agree that Pete and Milt were taking a whale of a beating. "Dixie, I think we'd better keep it at a walk or we'll kill 'em both for sure."

She also twisted around and followed his eyes. "Yeah," she said, "I'm afraid you're right. Did you believe him when he said that we might go to jail? Or that you could even be sentenced to hang!"

"Naw," Ruff scoffed. Then, as an afterthought, he added, "At least not as long as Milt keeps breathing."

Dixie stared at him. "I wish we were riding into Santa Fe instead of Rum River," she said, more to herself than to Ruff. "At least there we'd be assured of justice."

Ruff understood what his kid sister meant but chose not to add his own sentiments. Besides, he didn't really believe that he would be arrested for interfering with some two-bit horse shooters. Also, he had Dixie to witness that Milt would have gutted him like a deer if he hadn't shot the charging fool in the leg. He could just as easily have put a ball through Milt's lungs, same as the man had done to the poor bay mare he'd supposedly shot by accident. He would have left Milt lying beside the dead mustang as a warning to others that were as ruthless. But that aside, it was the reward on Blue Bullet that had captured Ruff's imagination.

"Dixie?"

"Yes?"

"Did you believe him about that thousand-dollar reward for the blue stallion?"

"Sure. Why else would he make up such a story? Or take

such a desperate chance if there was no reward?"

"I don't know," Ruff replied. "But if there really is a thousand-dollar reward, I think we ought to put our wits together and take a shot at it."

" 'Shot'?" Dixie wagged her pretty head back and forth. "Poor choice of words, Ruff."

"You understand what I meant."

"I do. But we don't know a damned thing about catching mustangs."

"We know horses. Mustangs or Thoroughbreds, a horse is a horse."

"Ha! I got a feeling that the only thing in common between, say, Blue Bullet and High Fire, is that they both like mares. Beyond that . . . I think they're as different as cats and dogs."

Ruff decided to chew on that awhile. He could talk a little horse in a special way, quite beyond the ability of most men. He could also read a Thoroughbred's mind, but perhaps Dixie was right about mustangs. They were wild as the wind. On the other hand, this Blue Bullet had once been owned and probably raced by this fella named Jack Grimm. And once tamed, Blue Bullet would remember the feel of a man and a saddle.

"What are you thinking about?" Dixie asked with suspicion.

"I'm just thinking that a thousand dollars' reward for the capture of that stallion would put us in high clover. Out in this country, we could buy a pretty fine piece of property with a house, barn, and corrals. We could really set ourselves up nice."

"Here in Rum River! What in the world would we do with racehorses in a valley overrun with cattle?"

Ruff could see her point. "All right, then, we could buy a spread somewhere around Santa Fe if we liked that country.

There's money in Santa Fe, Dixie. And I'm told they love horse races."

"From what I've seen so far of this New Mexico Territory, the smartest thing we can do is to dump these two men off and just keep riding."

Ruff disagreed. He liked this rugged New Mexico. True, it was mountainous and the winter snows were probably pretty deep at this elevation. But a man would have to ride a whole lot of country to find a valley or a community as shiny as Rum River.

And you didn't find a thousand dollars growing on pine trees.

They attracted a lot of attention riding into Rum River. Pete began to bellow for help while Milt, with his shattered leg, was a sobering sight. He looked dead and, Ruff thought, if they didn't find a competent doctor, he might soon be dead.

"Quit hollerin'!" Ruff ordered. "Where is the doctor in this town!"

"Ain't one, damn you! Just a tooth puller!"

"Where is he?" Ruff demanded a moment before he saw a sign that read: DR. BEN ZACKY. TOOTH EXTRACTIONS AND HAIRCUTS. CHEAP AND PAINLESS.

Ruff sighed. "He doesn't sound very competent, Dixie. What we really need is a first-class surgeon."

"We may have to go on to Santa Fe."

"Milt won't survive much longer. I think that Dr. Zacky is going to have to do."

Milt, overhearing them, yelped, "Zacky is the town drunk! You let him anywhere near Pete you'll swing for murder."

"Great," Ruff groused. "Just great."

"We might have to operate ourselves," Dixie said. "We've

done enough of it on horses to have a fair chance of saving Pete's life."

Ruff knew this was true. His father had been better than many college-educated surgeons during all the years he'd doctored his own Tennessee Thoroughbreds. And while most of his doctoring had been necessary during a foaling or to alleviate a colic, Justin had also kept a surgeon's instruments and had known how to skillfully use them. Very early on, he'd taught each of his children how to medicate a horse, then suture him up if he'd cut himself out in a paddock.

With a growing crowd of curious townspeople gathering in their wake, Ruff reined High Fire into a hitching post before Zacky's office and dismounted. Someone helped Pete down and the man collapsed in a pile. His bonds were cut and he had to be carried into the nearest saloon.

"You'll pay for this!" Pete screamed.

Ruff ignored Pete's threat. He motioned a spectator over and said, "This fella is heavy. Help me tote him into the doctor's office."

"He ain't there," the man said. "Probably over in the saloon getting his breakfast of rye whiskey."

"Then someone send for him!" Ruff snapped at the gawking crowd. "And if there's a sheriff in Rum River, tell him he'd better get over here right away."

"You tell him," a man said. "Here he comes."

Ruff had been about to bend over and try to lift Milt when he saw a fat man in his fifties with a shiny star on the front of his shirt come puffing up the street. The sheriff of Rum River was wearing a napkin poked into his belt and had obviously been eating because there were still wet gravy stains on his shirt. He was red faced with anger and exertion. There was a gun on his hip and the expression of extreme annoyance on his face.

"What's going on here! Who the hell are you!"

"My name is Rufus Ballou and this is my sister, Miss Dixie."

Ruff quickly explained about how he had seen Milt and Pete shoot the mustang mare and then intervened. He ended up by saying, "Sheriff, my sister will act as my witness. I ordered this one to halt but he just kept coming at me with his bowie knife. I finally had to shoot him in the leg out of self-defense. I could just have easily shot him dead."

"Oh, yeah!" the sheriff challenged in a belligerent tone of voice. "Well, who the hell do you think you are to shoot a man over nothin' more than a damned mustang!"

Ruff felt the hairs along the back of his neck rise. "Sheriff, where I come from, horses are considered worth more than a lot of people—and for a damned good reason. Now, I brought this man in and I'd like to see if we can save his life. So why don't you just hunt up Doc Zacky and let's see if he can be saved."

"Here comes Zacky!" someone shouted. "And he's still walking!"

When Ruff and Dixie turned to see the doctor, they were both appalled. Zacky was walking, all right, but not in a straight line. He was a tall, cadaverous man in his thirties with buck teeth and a black derby hat and a suit that looked as if it were stiff enough with grease and sweat to stand upright. Smoking the stub of a cheap cigar, he was having trouble focusing on the excitement gathered before his office.

"Gentlemen!" he hailed. "How kin I serve you."

"You can't," Dixie said, blocking the so-called doctor's path. "We need a surgeon, not a drunk!"

Zacky blinked. Tried to focus. "Miss . . ."

"Ballou."

"Well, Miss Ballou," Zacky said very carefully, "you

cannot always judge a book by its cover."

"I can when it smells like whiskey," she shot back. "We've a man with a shattered leg and you, sir, are not getting near him."

Zacky leaned forward on his toes, almost losing his balance as he tried to look over Dixie at the patient. Windmilling his arms, he regained his balance and said, "That man will die if I don't operate on his leg."

"Like my sister said," Ruff told the man, "you're drunk and unfit to operate on anything. We'll do the cutting if you've got the instruments."

"For a price, I will rent them to you," Zack said, looking only slightly offended. "Bring the patient into my operating parlor."

The "operating parlor" was nothing more than a dirty room with a barber's chair bolted to the floor. "Strap him down," Zacky ordered, "while I rustle up forceps, scalpel, and suture."

"In a barber's chair!"

"Works just fine," Zack told Ruff with a loose grin. "Pullin' a tooth or cuttin' a leg, either way you got to strap 'em down."

"Ruff?" Dixie asked, looking very worried.

"We've little choice," he said, struggling to drag Milt into the chair.

The sheriff, who had been momentarily forgotten, was now trying to show some authority. "All right, everyone out of here! This isn't any sideshow! Out!"

When the crowd finally retreated outdoors, the sheriff paused beside the door. Though the day was cool, he was sweating profusely. "By the way, mister, you're under arrest."

"What!"

The sheriff ignored Ruff's outburst. "As soon as we

know if the operation is successful or not, I'll know what the charges are. It'll either be for assault with a gun, or murder. Just don't try to sneak out the back door. I'll have a deputy waiting there with a shotgun. And just so you don't try to escape before turning yourself in, I'm confiscating your horses."

"You can't do that!"

"Sure I can! I'm Sheriff George Watson, and I can do damned near anything I jolly well want in Rum River."

Before either Dixie or Ruff could react, Watson slammed the office door. Behind Ruff, Doc Zacky burped and tripped over his own feet, crashing to the floor with a tray of dirty surgical instruments.

"We're in trouble," Ruff said.

"*Big* trouble."

Ruff nodded, then turned to study their unconscious patient strapped in the barber chair with his face the color of candle wax. At least, Ruff thought, there was one man in Rum River whose troubles outweighed their own.

THREE

Ruff had cut Milt's pant leg away and then propped the man's wounded leg up by resting his heel on a chair. Now he was poised with a scalpel while Dixie pressed a wet towel against the bullet wound.

"I sure don't want to do this," Ruff said, "but here goes."

When Ruff cut into the leg, Milt moaned but did not regain consciousness. Ruff quickly sliced down to the leg bone while Dixie applied pressure to the perimeter of the incision.

"First the ball," Ruff said, taking forceps and probing the wound until he felt metal touch metal. His heart was pounding and his brow was furrowed with concentration as he gently pinched the lead ball between the forceps and carefully extracted it. "There it is."

Ruff dropped the misshapen lead ball onto the floor. While he took a few deep, steadying breaths, Dixie applied pressure to staunch the bleeding. Behind them both, Doc Zacky watched with bloodshot eyes.

"You're a doctor, too?"

"Nope," Ruff said. "Well, maybe a horse doctor."

Zacky burped and grinned. "Horses? People? No damned difference 'cept their sizes. They're all made outta flesh, blood, and bone. Right?"

The doctor's fetid breath turned Ruff's stomach. "Why don't you just stumble back to the saloon and I'll come and get you when this is finished."

If Ruff's blunt suggestion offended the man, it did not show. Zacky said, "Nope. As a professional myself, I 'preciate good work."

Dixie rolled her brown eyes and lifted the towel. "What about the shattered bone?"

"I'll try and remove the loose fragments," Ruff told her. "But that's all we can do."

"Amputation?"

"Not a chance. He'd die of shock caused by blood loss. We'll just clean this up. Tie off the blood vessels we can find, then suture the muscle and skin. That's all we can do. The rest is up to God and how much this man wants to live."

"Thass right," Zacky agreed, bobbing his chin up and down. "God and guts! Thass what makes the difference."

"Get out of here!" Dixie stormed. "What kind of a doctor are you, drunk in the morning."

Zacky's had thick caterpillar-like eyebrows and now he did look offended. "Would ya prefer if I'd wait to get drunk until after lunch, miss?"

"I'd prefer that you just leave," Dixie said. "But not until you tell me who will look after this man while he mends."

"It'll cost you," Zacky gloated.

"All right, if he survives, how much?"

Zacky pursed his lips and tried to put his forefinger to them but missed his face. Clearing his throat and leaning against the barber chair, he said, "Oh, for a slight charge of, oh . . . a dollar a day. I'll watch over him."

"Not a chance."

"Then fin' someone on your own!" Zacky's eyes slitted with craftiness. "But before you do, I want . . . five dollars for the use of my surgical instruments and . . . and my operating parlor."

"You'll get a dollar," Ruff growled.

When Zacky stuck out his hand, palm open and up, Ruff had an almost overpowering desire to bury the scalpel into it. Instead, he wiped his hand off on the towel and found a dollar in his pocket, then paid Zacky. "Now git!"

"Hmmph!" Zacky wheeled around and navigated unsteadily toward the door. When he reached it, he fumbled with the knob, managed to get it open, and said, "That fella's a goner and you'll probably hang! I say good riddance to you both!"

Ruff actually would have hurled the scalpel at the fool but Dixie beat him to it with a pair of forceps, which struck Zacky in the chest. With a cry of outrage, the man staggered into the street. Dixie hurried over to close the door, then she went back to help Ruff tie off the bleeders and suture the leg.

It took almost an hour before Ruff straightened, feeling wrung out from tension. "It's finished," he told his sister. "All that we can do now is wait and see."

"What are we going to do about our horses?" Dixie asked, as they both slumped down on the floor. "We can't let Sheriff Watson have them."

"What choice do we have other than fighting our way out of this with guns?" Ruff asked. "Watson is determined to arrest and jail me. He must be up for reelection."

Tears welled up in Dixie's eyes and, despite everything she did to hide her feelings, a sob escaped her throat.

"Ah," Ruff said, wishing he hadn't been so depressingly candid, "it'll be all right. This fella is going to make it and the charges against me will be dismissed once everyone knows what really happened up in those mountains and how those fellas acted."

Dixie sniffled. "I got a bad feeling about this town. And from what little I've seen, people in this country don't seem to think the same way they do in Tennessee."

"If you mean that they don't respect horseflesh, I agree. But they will respect a man who shoots in self-defense."

Ruff waited a minute, then added, "Don't you think?"

"I just don't know," Dixie whispered. "But I'll tell you this much, I'll fight to the death before I let them steal our father's Thoroughbreds."

"So will I, but only as a last resort."

Ruff climbed wearily to his feet and helped his sister up as well. "Dixie, you've got to see that Milt survives so they don't charge me with murder. I'm going to visit the sheriff and see if I can't talk some sense into the man. It would be an injustice to confiscate our horses and send me to jail."

"I know that," Dixie said. "You know that. But the trouble is, the sheriff doesn't seem to know it."

"Let's just hope that the man has come to reason by now," Ruff said. "And as soon as I get this business settled, I think we ought to ride out of here and never look back."

"I agree!"

"Although," Ruff added with a wink of his eye, "I sure would like to try and have a run at that thousand-dollar reward for Blue Bullet. It sounds like easy money in the bank, given the speed of our two stallions."

"Ha!"

Ruff was pleased to see Dixie smile. And while he knew that things appeared bleak, it was his contention that, if a man didn't give up or go crazy, things would generally improve. To Ruff's way of thinking, life flowed like the seasons, good times alternating with bad times, successes and defeats. And it helped Ruff to understand that the bad times, like the good times, never lasted.

With that in mind, Ruff left his sister and went outside. "Which way is the sheriff's office?" he asked the first man he saw.

"Just up the street. Can't miss it for the smell."

"Much obliged," Ruff grunted, passing on.

A tough-looking young man with a fancy gun and a shiny badge fell in beside him. "I'm Deputy Bert Flagg and I'll be taking that sidearm. Raise your hands up nice and easy. Don't try anything dumb. Wouldn't bother me even a tad to put a hole in your belly."

Ruff saw a cruel challenge in the deputy's eyes. Not wanting to get into even more trouble, he decided to do as ordered. Without a word, he raised his hands and let Flagg take his Colt.

"You folks sure crowd an innocent man hard," Ruff told the deputy as they continued on toward the sheriff's office.

"We don't take to strangers shooting or beating up the locals, if that's what you mean."

"Oh, I get it," Ruff said, "but you do excuse horse killers."

Flagg's cheeks reddened. "Mister, you're just spoiling for a fall and it's commin'. People like you get what they deserve in Rum River."

Ruff clenched his teeth and bit back an angry reply. He was beginning to think everyone in this pretty little town was a half-cocked fool. So far, he'd yet to meet anyone with the sense that God had given a goose.

When they arrived at the sheriff's office, Ruff took a deep breath and said a little prayer that Sheriff Watson would be reasonable in the privacy of his own office. It was Ruff's experience that lawmen tended to overreact and show unnecessary authority when they were being watched by the public. Maybe they wanted to show off before the people who voted them into office.

"Did you disarm him?" Sheriff Watson asked, not even bothering to glance up from his paper.

"You bet!" Flagg smirked. "He could tell right away that I meant business."

Ruff's jaw muscles corded and it was all that he could do to squelch an unflattering remark. Instead, he surveyed the office and, given Sheriff Watson's own slovenly appearance, what he saw did not surprise him. The sheriff's office was a pigsty and obviously doubled as his living quarters. There was a pile of soiled clothing in one corner and discarded chicken bones in another. The lawman had his feet propped up on his scarred old desk and he finished reading his article before laying down his newspaper.

"Well, prisoner," the sheriff finally gloated, "I reckon you might even be smart enough to find your cell."

Ruff ignored the insult, took a deep breath, and said, "I think we need to have a little talk, Sheriff Watson. In the first place, there's no reason why I should be jailed. My sister will tell you that I acted in self-defense. Those men tried to shoot and then stab me. I could have killed them both, but I didn't."

Watson scratched, yawned, and smoothed his newspaper.

Ruff heard the deputy snicker but he ignored it and said to the sheriff, "So why don't we just admit that what happened up in those mountains was an unfortunate misunderstanding."

"Oh," the sheriff said, looking up at him again, "it was a hell of a lot more than just a 'misunderstanding.' You shot one citizen of this town and wounded another. Both Pete and Milt have a lot of friends in Rum River and those friends have long memories—and they vote."

Ruff felt like a man swimming against a strong tide. He wasn't getting anywhere with the sheriff and yet he had to keep trying. And maybe it was time to get right down to brass tacks. And though it galled him to pay extortion to a crooked lawman and his deputy, Ruff thought that might be the only way out of this fix.

"How much money would it take to convince you that I acted in self-defense?"

Watson barked a laugh. "Well, sir," he said, shooting a glance at his deputy, "there will be some expenses involved. First off, feed for you and those tall horses. Then there's our valuable time that is being spent on this case at the taxpayers' expense."

"What 'case'?" Ruff demanded.

"Why, *your* case, of course! And this office costs money to keep in operation. There are two salaries and . . . well, I think that those two stallions of yours would probably fetch about what it would cost to settle this matter out of court."

Ruff almost lunged for the man's throat. He hissed, "Go to hell. Both of you!"

The sheriff's grin died. A snarl twisted his lips and he dropped his boots to the floor and came to his feet, hands balled. "I could tell right away that you were a hardhead. Didn't I say that, Bert? That he was a hardhead."

"You sure did," Bert said, looking pleased.

"We got ways of dealing with hardheads."

"I want to see the judge!" Ruff stormed. "Right now."

"He's a traveling judge," the deputy said with a sinister smile. "A circuit judge. Won't be back this way for a while now. Too bad but you just missed him. Real shame."

Ruff knew they were trying to provoke him to attack so they could gun him down in cold blood. He was determined not to play their game and relaxed.

The sheriff looked disappointed. "Git into that cell before I have Deputy Flagg get rough."

Flagg grinned maliciously. He was about six feet tall, stocky, and had the appearance of a two-fisted brawler. The kind of man with even more pig iron in his fists than between his ears. The kind that would take two punches to deliver one. Ruff didn't want to fight the deputy, but neither did he want to go to jail or have his horses confiscated.

"Look," he said, trying one last time to strike an agreement, "between me and my sister, we have about seven dollars. Take it and let me and Dixie ride out of this town."

"Deputy? I seem to recall ordering this man into that cell yonder. And I seem to see him still standing here and arguing with me."

"I'll take care of that," Flagg said, driving a chopping uppercut into Ruff's side.

The pain was excruciating and Ruff folded. He barely had the presence of mind to block a second uppercut aimed at his chin. Then he whipped his own uppercut off the floor and caught Flagg moving forward. Flagg took the punch on the jaw, staggered, shook off the effects of the blow, and waded in on Ruff with both fists.

It was a hard fight as Ruff stood toe to toe with the deputy while the excited sheriff yelled, "Git him! Hook 'em! Drop him!"

Ruff could sense that he was losing. His blows punished and marked the deputy but they lacked their usual power, and he felt weakened from his earlier fight with Milt. Ruff found himself backing up as Deputy Flagg pounded at him with both fists. Realizing that he was going to be knocked senseless, Ruff swept his foot out, catching Flagg behind the knees and toppling him to the floor.

Before the deputy could bounce up, Ruff grabbed Flagg by the ears and drove his knee into the deputy's face. The fight was over.

"Hands up!" Sheriff Watson screamed, drawing and cocking the hammer of his six-gun. "One move and I'll blow you straight to hell!"

Ruff raised his hands. The sheriff's expression was wild with hatred and his eyes were crazy. "Just take it easy," Ruff said, moving toward the filthy cell. "I'm unarmed."

"I wish you did have a gun in that holster! I'd riddle you like a damned cheese!"

Ruff not only entered the cell, but he slammed and locked the door behind him, deciding that it was the wisest possible move he could make, given the circumstances.

When the cell door clicked shut, Watson jumped forward, snatching keys off his desk. He locked the door and his face was the color of a radish. "If you broke that boy's face, I swear I'll gun you down. Claim you was trying to escape."

Ruff sat down on an empty whiskey barrel knowing how very close he was to death. Watson and his deputy were two of a kind—both men liked to inflict pain, exercise authority, and were plenty capable of conducting a private execution.

"Just relax and take it easy," Ruff said, forcing a smile. "No need to use that gun, Sheriff."

The Colt trembled in Watson's pudgy fist and Ruff's heart stopped beating for a moment as the balance scale of reason tipped one way and then the other. But at last, the sheriff holstered his gun and went to the aid of his young deputy.

Bert Flagg was conscious, but just barely. Blood was streaming down his face and Ruff knew he'd broken the man's nose. He also knew that, given Flagg's twisted nature, there would be hell to pay when the deputy regained his senses.

Ruff leaned back against his cell wall and closed his eyes. He couldn't believe how fast things could go bad. Twenty-four hours ago, he and Dixie had been up in the beautiful Sangre de Cristo Mountains enjoying the most spectacular scenery that God had ever put on this good earth. Now, here he was in a stinking cell in Rum River with two lawmen who would make his life a living hell.

FOUR

Dixie had found a part-time job mucking out stalls as well as grooming horses so that she would have enough money to feed herself as well as be near the Ballou Thoroughbreds. But the work didn't even pay enough to offset the feed bills being accumulated against their four horses, and Dixie was hoping to find full-time employment. She'd gone to every business in town, but so far, nothing. And each day that passed put her and Ruff deeper into debt.

Dixie visited Ruff three times a day in his filthy cell. Out of her own meager earnings, she brought him a little extra food, sometimes a pastry as a treat. Anything to brighten his spirits. She even brought Ruff buckets of hot, soapy water and a scrub brush so that he could clean his cell as well as himself. And each time, she never missed a chance to take a verbal swipe at Sheriff George Watson.

"This place is worse than a pigpen," she'd say. "Why don't you clean it up? Why, don't you clean *yourself* up?"

"Shut up," Watson would growl. "Before I get mad enough to arrest and throw you in jail along with your brother."

"On what charges?"

"Give me a minute and I'll damn sure think of something, little sassy britches."

And before he really did, Dixie would return to the livery where she consoled herself by being around her beautiful Thoroughbreds. Never before had High Fire, High Man, and the their two gentle brood mares had such a good daily brushing.

One day the livery owner, Mr. Jed Dobler, a kind man who walked with a cane from being stomped by a bronc years earlier, called to her, "Dixie, come on outside. Mr. Grimm would like to meet you."

Dixie laid her curry comb down beside High Fire's stall and brushed back her hair. She whacked the dust off her shirt and pants, then polished her boots on the backs of her pant legs. Everyone knew that Jack Grimm was the power in Rum River. And though Dixie had no idea what the man wanted of her, she hoped that something good might come of the introduction.

Stepping out of the barn into the sunlight, Dixie beheld a dapper-looking gentleman riding a beautiful bay Thoroughbred stallion. Unlike every westerner that Dixie had seen since leaving the South, Jack Grimm was riding an English saddle and wearing English boots and jodhpurs. He looked very out of place in New Mexico but he was so attractive a horseman that his mere presence commanded immediate respect. In his thirties, his face was tanned and his teeth were a flash of white over a square jaw and cleft chin. And although he wasn't a big man, he exuded virility and confidence.

"Good afternoon, Miss Ballou. I've heard that you and your brother have gotten into a bit of a fix here in Rum River."

Dixie was momentarily taken aback by such a direct statement. "Why . . . yes. There has been a terrible misunderstanding."

"I hope so, for your brother's sake," Grimm said, dismounting and tossing his reins to Mr. Dobler as if he were one of his own stable hands. "I understand that you and your brother also own some fine Thoroughbred horses."

"That's right," Dixie said, measuring both the man and his horse and judging them equally impressive.

"May I have the opportunity to view them?" Grimm asked. He made a sweeping gesture toward his stallion. "As you can see, I also love the breed."

"That's a magnificent stallion."

"He is that," Grimm said. "Do your horses have any track record, so to speak?"

The question was posed in a most casual manner but Dixie wasn't a bit fooled. She had watched her brother and father handle such inquiries hundreds of times. The more casual the question, the more likely that it was the inquirer had a keen interest in either buying a Ballou Thoroughbred or racing against it for money.

"Yes," Dixie said, "our older stallion, High Man, was raced quite often in his prime. His son, High Fire, is four years old but he's had some minor leg problems. He's sound, but . . . well, you know how this rough country is on a purebred horse, Mr. Grimm."

"Oh, I do! I do! However, if a Thoroughbred has the proper breeding infused in his lineage, he can stand up quite nicely to this country, Miss Ballou. Out here, we breed for bone as well as for speed. That's the secret of my success."

"I'm sure it is," Dixie said, feeding the man's pride before adding, "that must be why Blue Bullet has adapted so well in the wild. I understand that he once belonged to you."

Grimm's smile evaporated like fog in sunlight. His eyes narrowed. "Blue Bullet still belongs to me, Miss Ballou. And one of these days, I shall have him back."

"I'm sure you will," Dixie said with an innocent smile, "if he isn't shot to death first."

Grimm had been about to say something, but now he started. "What is that remark supposed to mean?"

Dixie sensed she had touched a nerve ending. She applied pressure. "Haven't you heard what those two men were trying to do in order to collect the reward you are offering?"

"No." Grimm leaned forward, his expression hard and intense. "What are you talking about, Miss Ballou?"

"I'm talking about those men attempting to crease Blue Bullet's neck in order to stun him. Once stunned, they hoped to reach Blue Bullet before he revived, and hobble and bring him in for your reward."

Grimm's blinked with surprise. His jaw muscles corded. "Are you sure! No one has said any such thing to me."

"I'm glad to hear that," Dixie said truthfully. "Because it doesn't take a lot of brain power to imagine how poor the chances are of merely creasing or nicking a horse's spinal cord. Even with a marksman, the odds must be a hundred to one. Maybe higher. Be a terrible shame to kill an animal as magnificent as Blue Bullet. The poor mare shot by accident was also a fine animal."

Grimm's face darkened with anger. "Have you any proof of what you are saying?"

"It's our word against theirs," Dixie said. "But why else would we have gotten into such a bad fix? Both Ruff and I were outraged. You see, where we come from, such a practice would qualify a man for a lynching."

Grimm threw a glance at Mr. Dobler and said, "Jed? Have you heard this story before?"

"No," the liveryman replied, "but it doesn't surprise me. How long have you had that standing reward on Blue Bullet? Must be over a year now. No one can catch that stallion or his band of mares. I think that Milt and Pete just figured that one chance in a hundred was better than no chances."

Grimm turned away, his handsome face twisted with anger. "Is Milt still over at the Zacky's?"

"No," Dixie said. "They've moved him to Fletcher's Boarding House. Mrs. Fletcher is watching over him. His recovery is coming along better than anyone had hoped."

"I see." Grimm was thoughtful a moment before he seemed to remember that Dixie was present. "Miss Ballou, I understand that you and your brother actually operated on his leg."

"We didn't want to, but there wasn't much choice, given Doc Zacky's sorry condition."

"Where did you learn to practice medicine?"

"In Tennessee, where our father raised Thoroughbreds. He always said that by the time a horseman could get a veterinarian out, a seriously ill or injured horse would already be dead. So he taught us a lot of good, practical medicine."

Jack Grimm nodded. "Your father sounds like he was a very intelligent man. It's a shame that you and your brother have gotten yourself in such a mess."

"As a lover of fine horses, I'm sure that you of all people understand how outraged we were when we saw those two men shooting at Blue Bullet and his mustang mares. Are the mares yours, also, Mr. Grimm?"

"Yes," he said with a shake of his head. "I'm afraid so. That stallion has been worse than a plague for me and my horse-breeding program. But you know what . . . the more he steals from me, the more I want him back."

"Why?" Dixie pointedly asked.

Their eyes locked for a moment and then the rancher smiled. "Blue Bullet is this bay stallion's half brother, Miss Ballou. And when they were colts in the same pasture, they used to race and play together. And you know what?"

"I think I can guess." Dixie moved around Grimm's bay stallion. "This is a fine animal, but Blue Bullet is one in a million. Unless I miss my guess, Blue Bullet used to routinely outrun this horse. Isn't that true, Mr. Grimm?"

He laughed, clearly amused. "You're smart, Miss Ballou. Very smart. Yes. The blue always beat Cannonade. And there's something in me that has always demanded the best and the fastest. Maybe your father felt the same way."

"Not only my father, but my brothers and myself," she told the man. "That's why we brought the last and the best of our Thoroughbreds west."

He studied her for a long moment, eyes bold and measuring. Dixie felt her cheeks warm. He was not old enough to be her father, and his eyes told her he thought he was young enough to be her lover. They reflected admiration at her budding contours.

"Jed, why don't you grain and curry Cannonade. I'll pick him up after I've visited with Miss Ballou and had a chance to look at her horses."

"Yes, sir," Jed Dobler said, displaying nothing of his feelings.

"You working for Jed?" Grimm asked as they moved side by side into the barn.

"Yes."

"I doubt he can afford to pay you what you're really worth, Miss Ballou. I could use you myself out at the ranch. All I can find in this country are cowboys. They can ride a wildcat but they're too rough for purebreds. They've no patience or interest in bringing a high-spirited horse along carefully."

"That doesn't surprise me," Dixie said. "People out in this country lack sensitivity around purebred horses."

"I couldn't have put it better myself if I'd tried," he said agreeably, "and I think you'd fit into my plans perfectly and appreciate the quality of Thoroughbreds I'm raising. I'll pay you well."

"Thanks, but no, thanks," Dixie said. "I need to stay close to my brother."

"From what I hear," Grimm said, "your brother isn't going anywhere. My ranch is only about three miles up the road. You could exercise my Thoroughbreds by galloping them into Rum River to visit the jail."

He was pressing her and Dixie didn't like that. "I'll think about it," she hedged, coming up to the first stall. "This is our foundation sire, High Man. Many years ago, my father won his sire, High Dancer, playing a high-stakes card game in Richmond, Virginia."

The interior of the barn was dim and the New Mexico rancher squinted, leaning over the door into the stall for a good look. "He's a big, fine-looking animal. How old is he?"

"Eighteen years old and he can still run like the wind," Dixie said, unable to mask the pride in her voice.

"I'm sure he can," Grimm said, his voice patronizing.

She moved over to the brood mares. "These girls are eight and ten. They've thrown some fine colts and fillies."

"I'd like to see them better," Grimm said. "Mind bringing them out of their stalls?"

"Not at all." Dixie haltered and brought each mare out, then paraded her around the barn.

"Very, very nice," Grimm said, his voice no longer patronizing. "Fine-looking mares. Are they for sale?"

"I'm afraid not."

Dixie put the mares away and went to bring out their young stallion, High Fire. The moment that Jack Grimm saw the tall sorrel Thoroughbred with the blazed face and four white stockings, he became almost animated.

"That is one *hell* of a horse! Now I'd really be interested in buying him."

"Not for sale at any price," Dixie said, scratching High Fire's neck.

"Oh, come on!" Grimm said, forcing a laugh. "Everything has a price."

"Not these horses. You see, they represent my father's life work. You can't put a price on something like that, Mr. Grimm. That's why we'd never sell any of these horses. But in a few years, Ruff and I hope to establish our own horse ranch, perhaps even up around Santa Fe. If the war is still on, we'll provide a few Thoroughbreds to the Confederacy. If the war is over, we'd be willing to sell our offspring to qualified buyers such as yourself."

"I see," Grimm said, unable to hide his disappointment. "How fast is that stallion?"

"Very fast."

Grimm chuckled. "You interested in a horse race?"

"I'm interested in getting my brother out of jail," Dixie bluntly replied. "If you can help me do that, then—"

"I can't," he interrupted. "It's not a matter that I have any control over."

Dixie tried to hide her disappointment. She put High Fire away and then came back to stand before the rancher and Thoroughbred breeder. "Mr. Grimm, I think you have control over almost everything that happens in Rum River. I'd like you to try and get my brother out of jail. I'm very worried about Sheriff Watson and Deputy Flagg. Both are determined to make my brother's life as miserable as possible."

Grimm placed his hand on Dixie's shoulder and squeezed it gently. "Miss Ballou," he said, moving a little closer, "I don't know if it will help, but I'll speak to the sheriff and his deputy and then to your brother. It seems to me that your brother might have been provoked to the same violent reaction I'd have felt if I had seen those men shooting at the mustangs."

Dixie was so grateful that she wanted to throw her arms around this wealthy man and give him a big hug. Instead, she swallowed a lump in her throat and managed to say,

"I'm extremely grateful, Mr. Grimm."

"Jack," he said gently. "Please call me Jack."

"All right, Jack. And I'd like you to call me Dixie."

"Well, Dixie," he said, turning to leave, "if I can't buy that four-year-old stallion or any of your brood mares, perhaps we can at least have us a friendly horse race."

"It would have to be 'friendly,' " Dixie told him. "You see, Ruff and I are pretty near broke. That's why I'm working here in the mornings."

"And why," he said, turning at the doorway, "you need to come to work for me, full-time. And then, after we've convinced the judge to set your brother free, we can really talk business."

Dixie knew that charming, handsome Jack Grimm was drawing her into his web of influence, but there was no point of resisting as long as her brother was in jail. Dixie was scared to death that the sheriff or his deputy would find a way to murder her brother out of pure meanness and spite. Deputy Flagg's face was a mess, his broken nose purple and grossly swollen. A proud, rash man like that with the power of a lawman's badge was very unstable and dangerous. Dixie knew that no matter what risks she might be getting into by going out to work for Jack Grimm, it was something that she had to do for Ruff.

To do nothing and play it safe was unthinkable. "All right, Jack," she heard herself tell him, "when would you like me to start?"

"How does tomorrow sound? It would give us both time to make arrangements."

"That would be perfect. However, there is one thing."

"And that is?"

"I'd like to bring our horses out to your ranch," Dixie said. "Even though I like and trust Mr. Dobler, I can't take the chance that someone wouldn't try to hurt or steal them."

"You *are* concerned, aren't you."

"You would be, too, if you knew how fast High Fire can run," Dixie said.

Jack raised his eyebrows and grinned. "I intend to find out," he said. "Believe me, I intend to find out."

He left her at the door, saying, "I'll send a couple of men over tomorrow morning for you and your horses."

"That won't be necessary, Jack. In fact, I can't allow anyone else to handle my horses. I know that you'll understand."

Grimm frowned, indicating that he did not understand. However, it was equally obvious that he did not wish to create an issue. Instead, he gestured up the street. "I'm going to pay a little visit to the sheriff's office. I want to talk to your brother and then to the sheriff and his deputy."

"Thank you."

He grinned. "Just a talk, Miss Ballou. Nothing more. But is there any message I can give your brother?"

"Tell him that I'll be along later. And, Jack?"

"Yes," he said, turning back.

"Please don't tell him that I've agreed to come to work for you. It would be best if I told him myself."

"Certainly. I understand. He feels responsible for you and those outstanding horses. Yes, I can see where it would be better if you told him yourself."

Dixie smiled and stuck out her hand. She had heard that Jack Grimm could be a tyrant and was extremely ruthless. Maybe that was all true, but she also believed in her heart that he loved fine horses and had been genuinely outraged to learn the truth of what Milt and Pete had attempted.

"Tomorrow morning, then," he said, turning and walking up the street.

Dixie watched him greet almost everyone he saw. She tried to judge whether people were pleased or intimidated by Jack Grimm. One thing was for certain, the rancher and Thoroughbred horse raiser was going to have a few choice words for Milt and Pete the next time he saw them. And so, for the first time since arriving in Rum River, Dixie felt a glimmer of hope.

FIVE

Ruff was feeling lower than a frog's butt when Jack Grimm stepped into the sheriff's office. Watson was in his usual position with his feet propped up on his desk. He was dozing with the newspaper stretched out across his bloated belly like a dirty linen napkin. Deputy Bert Flagg was off somewhere making rounds.

Without warning, Jack Grimm grabbed the sheriff's boots and hurled them sideways. Watson spun on his deck chair and cried out with alarm. When his chair swung around, the sheriff slid out and crashed to the floor, sputtering and trying to gather his wits.

"Wake up, you fat fool!" Grimm snapped, eyes raking the sheriff with disgust. "What the hell kind of a lawman are you, George!"

Before George could answer, Grimm kicked the door open wide. "Christ, this place stinks! I swear you're a hog and by damned I'm going to leave this door open and tell everyone about it! Come election time, I'll roast your fat carcass and send you packing!"

Watson was a pathetic sight as he struggled to his feet, still half-asleep and in a state of near panic. "Please, Mr. Grimm! I worked late last night. I was just catchin' a nap. That's all!"

From behind cell bars, Ruff could not help but smile. No one had to tell him who this visitor was and why he was yanking the sheriff's strings as if he were a cheap, overstuffed puppet. Ruff didn't know why Jack Grimm was so much on the prod, but it was a pleasure to watch the sheriff bear the brunt of the rancher's anger.

"I swear, George. If that deputy of yours had an ounce of sense, I'd have used him to replace you long ago!"

"Oh, Mr. Grimm! You can't mean that! After all my years of loyal—"

"Shut up and get out of here," Grimm growled. "You make me sick to my stomach. Go jump in a water trough if you won't take a bath! Just get out of my sight while I have a talk with your prisoner."

"Mr. Grimm, he's a mean one! You'd best be careful!"

"Out!"

The sheriff whirled and shambled through the door, the newspaper flying in his wake. Jack Grimm watched him scuttle across the street and then he turned and shook his head.

Glancing at Ruff, he said, "As you can plainly see, it's hard to find good help anymore."

Ruff didn't quite know what to say to that. So he just nodded his head and waited to see which way the wind was going to blow. Two things were immediately apparent. Grimm owned not only the community of Rum River, but also its law. It seemed quite reasonable to assume that he might also own the territorial circuit judge.

Grimm righted the sheriff's office chair and dragged it over before the cell. Before he sat down, he studied Ruff and then he jammed his hand through the bars and said, "My name is Jack Grimm. Yours is Rufus Ballou."

Ruff took the rancher's hand. He was surprised that it was callused. Grimm had the appearance of a man who'd never raised so much as an honest sweat in his entire life, but his calluses said different.

"My pleasure, Mr. Grimm."

"Jack. You work for me, you call me Mr. Grimm. Otherwise, Jack."

"All right, then, Jack."

The man studied Ruff. "How old are you?"

Ruff was aware that he cut a pretty sorry figure compared to this wealthy, domineering man. "I'm nineteen."

"You look about five years older. How old is your sister?"

"Fifteen. Why do you ask?"

"Just curious. I met her a few minutes ago over at Dobler's Livery. Nice girl."

"So what did you and Dixie have to talk about?"

"Horses. Thoroughbred horses. I like yours very much but your sister says that they're not for sale."

"She says right."

"There's a price on everything." Grimm flashed a perfect smile. "I don't know what yours is yet, but I intend to find out."

"There is no price," Ruff repeated.

"Bullshit!" Grimm lowered himself into the chair and relaxed as he regarded Ruff. "You're in a real fix. You're horse rich and dollar poor."

"Not so poor we can't get out of this scrape," Ruff vowed. "My sister and I hail from Tennessee. We've lost two brothers and a father and had more than our share of fights. We don't quit when things get tough."

"You're not in Tennessee any longer, Reb. You're in New Mexico and you're in jail. Think about that. Think about a judge who hates the South and about the charges that you're facing."

Ruff gripped the cell bars. He knew that he had no cards to play and he also knew that it would be very stupid to argue with someone who controlled the game. "I've been thinking about little else," he confessed. "And I know I'm in a fix."

"Yes, you are."

"Did Dixie tell you what happened? Why I shot Milt in the leg and whipped Pete?"

"She did."

Ruff studied the man, still not able to read his mind. "Well, then," he said finally, "you raise Thoroughbreds. That being the case, I'll assume you and I share a mutual respect for quality horseflesh. So what would you have done if you'd seen a couple of fellas shooting at a band of mustangs for no apparent reason except to kill them?"

"I'd have probably shot the bastards dead and left them for the buzzards," Grimm announced.

Ruff blinked. "You would have?"

"That's right. Especially if I'd have realized why they were firing. When your sister told me about them trying to crease Blue Bullet's neck, it was all I could do not to march down to the boardinghouse and break Milt's other leg! And I might still do it."

Ruff expelled a deep breath. "Well, I'll be," he said with a broad smile.

"Listen," Grimm said, "I feel somewhat responsible for the fix you're in because it was my reward that brought men to such desperate measures of trying to crease Blue Bullet. So, as of this very moment, I'm going to put out the word that there'll be no reward for any man who fires on the mustangs."

"That'd help the mustangs, all right," Ruff conceded.

"Yes, but it won't help you." Grimm frowned. "I do happen to be counted among Judge Pointer's best friends. And I'm going to have a talk with him before he passes sentence on you."

"Why don't you simply explain what happened and then ask him to dismiss the charges," Ruff said, disappointed at the offer.

Grimm shrugged and looked Ruff straight in the eyes.

"Like I said before, *everything* has a price."

Ruff squeezed the bars of his cell until his knuckles turned white. "I understand," he said. "But no deal. Our horses are not for sale."

"Sure," Grimm said, removing a cigar from his coat pocket, nipping off the tip with a pair of silver clippers, then lighting it thoughtfully. "So what about a horse race?"

"We've got nothing to wager and I wouldn't let Dixie race unless I'm present."

"I think I can get you an afternoon's reprieve from this cell in order to oversee the race."

"We don't have any money to wager," Ruff said. "I'm sure you've guessed that much."

"Then we'll bet horse against horse."

When Ruff hesitated, Grimm smiled. "I've seen your stallion, High Fire. You haven't seen mine, Cannonade, so I understand your reluctance. But your sister has seen my bay Thoroughbred. Why don't you talk to her and decide?"

When Ruff didn't respond, Grimm chuckled. "Listen, no matter who wins it will be a race long remembered. I'll set it up for Sunday. That will give us a few days to get the word out so we'll have four or five hundred spectators all wagering. Some of the bigger-money boys will come from as far away as Santa Fe. We'll race a mile, right through the center of Rum River. Give everyone a hell of a treat. If you win, you've my word that charges will be dismissed and you can ride off with Cannonade, a horse that will bring you a minimum of one thousand dollars."

"But if we lose?"

Grimm shrugged. "I'll still guarantee that the charges are dismissed. You'll lose your four-year-old stallion, but you'll still have the old one and the brood mares. Besides, why would you want to keep a loser?"

Ruff stepped back from the bars. This wasn't his kind

of game. In the first place, Grimm was setting all the terms. Distance, place, and method of running the race. No doubt, Grimm would stage a few unwelcome distractions and surprises along the way, giving Cannonade a big edge. On the other hand, the length of the town itself was only a few hundred yards so there would be a lot of open track on either end of Rum River where Dixie could let High Fire run free.

"I'll talk to my sister."

"Good!" The rancher leaned back in the sheriff's desk chair and regarded Ruff thoughtfully. After a minute, he said, "Did you fight in the war?"

"No," Ruff admitted. "I wanted to sign up, but I was the youngest son and my father refused. He'd already lost his two oldest sons."

"So you got lucky."

"Not the way I figure it," Ruff said with a sigh of regret. "I had to watch my father get shot down by a Confederate officer who was too foolish to take no for an answer when he demanded the last of our Thoroughbreds. I buried him and another brother named John near Missionary Ridge. My closest brother, Houston, is rotting in a federal prison. Our family name is a curse word in Tennessee and all I have left in this world is my sister and those four horses."

Ruff scowled. "And right now, I'm wondering what kind of a game you're trying to play on me, Mr. Grimm. I'll be honest: I don't trust you."

"Ha!" Grimm laughed. "Why should you! I've no use for Rebs and I want that sorrel stallion. At least, if he's as fast as your sister says he is, I do."

"And you want Blue Bullet," Ruff said. "And all I want is to get out of this jail and to claim that thousand-dollar reward you're offering."

"You can have both—if you win. Relaying our two stallions, you ought to be able to run Blue Bullet into the ground. That is, if you are horseman enough."

"I could handle it," Ruff said. He studied Grimm's handsome face. "Just let me tell you one thing, Jack. If we race, my sister will be riding High Fire and I won't stand for any shenanigans. Especially those that might endanger my sister. Is that understood?"

"Don't threaten me," Grimm said, blowing smoke in Ruff's face. "You're in no position for it. Besides, I share your respect for fast horses and I like your sister—very much."

Ruff didn't like the way he said that but he believed the man.

"I hope," Grimm said as he pushed out of his chair and started to leave, "that you'll have the courage to agree to this race. I have always enjoyed competing against the best."

"Will you ride your own horse, or hire some midget to ride him for you?"

Grimm laughed outright. "Why, I'll ride him myself, since it seems to be an issue."

The measure of the man elevated in Ruff's eyes and as far as he was concerned, the race would take place if Dixie was willing to make the ride and risk their great young stallion.

Jack Grimm left but less than twenty minutes later, Sheriff Watson came rushing into the office, pale and obviously shaken. The first thing he did was to yank open his desk drawer and extract a full fifth of whiskey. Upending the bottle, he drank deeply, then sighed and ran his hands across his sweating face.

Glancing over at Ruff, he yelled, "What are you staring at!"

"A man who looks like he's seen a ghost. What's wrong,

Sheriff? Some little kid steal a piece of candy and now you have to face him down?"

"Shut up!" Watson took another swig of whiskey and glared at Ruff. "Do you have any idea what just happened?"

"No," Ruff said. "I'm a little out of touch with things in Rum River, as you might imagine."

Ignoring the sarcasm, Sheriff Watson blurted, "Mr. Grimm hunted up Milt. When he found him, he walked up and kicked Milt square in his shot leg! Right smack dab on the bullet hole. Jeezus! Everyone in town heard Milt scream. Mr. Grimm dragged Milt out of bed, threw him to the floor, and stomped that leg three more times with Milt howlin' like a coyote at the moon."

The sheriff took another drink. "By the time I arrived, I thought Milt was being butchered. Then Mr. Grimm, he said he would kill Milt or anyone else who shot at Blue Bullet or his band of mustang mares."

"How is Milt?"

"He was bleeding pretty bad when Doc Zacky arrived. I don't know what's going to happen. Mr. Grimm went to the livery and got his horse, then rode back to his ranch."

Ruff turned his back on the sheriff and went over to peer out his little cell window that faced the alley. He couldn't see anything, but at least the sheriff wouldn't be able to note the deep concern on his face. What kind of a man would stomp the broken leg of another human being? Even a human being as vile as Milt? Maybe, Ruff thought, he should forget about the horse race. Anyone ruthless enough to do what Jack Grimm had done to Milt was not to be trusted.

And yet, Ruff knew he really had no choice. If he refused the race he was either going to be shot or sent to prison.

• • •

That evening, Dixie brought Ruff an entire apple pie and a jug of coffee. She looked excited and hopeful. "What did you think of Jack?"

Ruff took a big bite of the pie and chewed it thoughtfully. "I think he loves Thoroughbred horses but will stop at nothing to get what he wants. And what he wants is whatever he hasn't got."

Dixie's smile faded. "You think he's pretty bad, huh?"

"Did you hear what he did to Milt's leg?"

"Yes," Dixie said, lowering her eyes. "And I'll admit I was as shocked as everyone else. I went over to help Doc Zacky. He was actually sober. We managed to get the bleeding stopped and I think that Milt will recover, though the bone probably was rebroken. It was a terrible punishment."

"Jack Grimm, underneath those fancy clothes and manners, is utterly ruthless. Did he tell you that he wants to race High Fire?"

"In so many words."

"What do you think?"

"What are the stakes?"

Ruff told her, then asked, "What is your impression of his stallion?"

"Cannonade is magnificent," Dixie conceded. "He's almost seventeen hands tall and powerfully built. I think he can probably run like a machine."

"So," Ruff said, suppressing a grin, "you think our horse can beat him."

"Yes. But then, we both think High Fire can outrun anything on four legs over a mile. Isn't that right?"

Ruff nodded. "Grimm wants to race next Sunday."

"I wish it were tomorrow so you could be free."

"Me, too," Ruff said. "But you know what. I think,

despite Grimm's brutal ways, he's a man of his word. And so, I think he will talk to the judge and I'll be released, win, lose, or draw."

"Then let's race!" Dixie urged.

"Okay. We'll do it."

Dixie clasped his hand. "There is one other think that we need to talk about. I want to go to work for Jack."

"Absolutely not!"

"Ruff, we need the money!"

"No!" Ruff lowered his voice. "In addition to worrying about you out there, who would watch our horses?"

"I'd take them with me. Jack said that would be fine."

"Not a chance."

"Ruff, please! It will give me a better idea of what kind of a man we're up against."

"We already know that," Ruff argued. "Jack is the kind that would viciously stomp another's broken leg! Dixie, this guy is dangerous! He'll do whatever it takes to get what he wants. And besides High Fire, I think he has his eyes on you!"

Dixie looked away, color coming to her face.

"So," Ruff said, "You felt that desire, too, didn't you."

"Yes," Dixie whispered, "but I can handle him."

"Oh, no, you can't. Dixie, please. We're going to have enough to worry about winning that race. Stay in Rum River."

"But what about the money, Ruff? If I go to work for Mr. Grimm, even for a week and a half, I'll have a few dollars coming to pay off our livery bill. But if not . . ."

"Dixie, I swear we'll find a way to settle our debts. Even if we have to sell our saddles to do it, we'll leave this town owing no one. Maybe we'll even ride out with Cannonade and a thousand dollars of reward money for Blue Bullet in our pockets."

Dixie sighed. "All right," she said. "I'll tell Mr. Grimm that I've changed my mind now that I know we're going to race him stallion for stallion. But he won't be pleased."

"To hell with him!" Ruff snapped. "Whether or not he's pleased means nothing to us. All that matters now is winning the race and hoping that Grimm keeps his word and gets me out of this jail."

"Yes," Dixie said quietly. "And if we should lose?"

Ruff scowled. "If we lose, we lose. We'd keep High Fire and he's still capable of siring great horses. It wouldn't be the end of the world, Dixie. And as Father used to say, 'In a horse race, expect the unexpected.' "

Dixie dipped her chin and said, "Do you like the pie I brought?"

"It's wonderful. Want some?"

"No, thanks."

Ruff ate the pie and it was delicious. Ruff tried to restore Dixie's good humor but failed. He knew how worried his sister was about their mounting livery and other debts. And about the horse race. But worrying didn't help things even a little bit. All that they could do from now until the horse race was to see that High Fire received plenty of feed and exercise and didn't go off his diet.

After that, the race was up for grabs and may the best horse win.

SIX

The next morning, as promised, a buggy and two riders arrived from the Grimm Ranch to fetch Dixie and the Ballou Thoroughbreds. Dixie met them at the stable with more than a little anxiety.

"I'm afraid that I won't be able to go to work for Mr. Grimm," she said to the man in charge. "I've changed my mind. I'm staying in Rum River."

"That's not what Mr. Grimm told us," the man said, dismounting. "My name is Dick Hastings. I'm the foreman and my boss's orders are to bring you and Tennessee horses to his ranch. So that's what we mean to do."

"Now, wait a minute, Mr. Hastings," Dixie said with amazement. "Didn't you understand? I've changed my mind."

"Tell it to Mr. Grimm," the foreman said, seizing her wrist and gently but firmly pulling her toward the buggy.

Dixie reared back and bashed Hastings in the jaw with her fist. He lifted her into the buggy. "Halter her Thoroughbreds, get her luggage from the hotel, and bring everything along!" he yelled to his men while a companion pinned Dixie between them.

"Are you crazy!" Dixie shouted as the buggy carried them away. "You can't abduct someone against their will!"

"Sure we can," the man who was holding Dixie grunted. "Now, you'd best hold still and enjoy the short ride. In less than a mile, we'll be on the Grimm Ranch. The mansion is about two miles farther and it's a sight you won't soon forget."

53

"Damn!" Dixie cussed. "You fools are going to pay for this!"

"If we didn't follow the boss's orders, then we'd pay, that's for certain," Hastings drawled.

There was no use in struggling any longer so Dixie resigned herself to being hauled out to meet Jack Grimm against her will. Once there, she meant to give the rancher and these employees an earful. This was disgraceful!

But a short time later, when Dixie saw the huge and impressive horse and cattle ranch, she calmed down a little. Jack Grimm was raising purebred Black Angus cattle, a short but hearty breed from Scotland. They were beautiful, with shiny ebony coats. There were at least five hundred grazing in irrigated pastures divided by white wooden fences. Even more impressive was a small herd of buffalo. They were immense, shaggy beasts, larger than oxen.

"You've never seen buffalo before, have you?" the ranch foreman asked.

"No."

"Mr. Grimm had 'em imported from Wyoming, Colorado, and Nebraska. There's still plenty of wild buffalo runnin' loose, but they're bein' slaughtered by the tens of thousands for nothing but their hides. Mr. Grimm says that in twenty years or less, there probably won't be any more. The reason he imported them from three different states is so there will be no inbreeding."

"Where are his Thoroughbreds?"

"Up closer to the ranch house. I think you'll be glad that we made you come, Miss Ballou. Your Thoroughbreds will sure have it a lot better here than in town. Mr. Grimm feeds the finest hay and grain that money can buy. Everything is first class. I'll guarantee that you won't see anything the equal of this place in the West."

Dixie could already see that this was true. It was obvious

that Jack Grimm was wealthy beyond measure and had not made his fortune raising livestock or Thoroughbreds.

"What did Mr. Grimm do, find a gold mine on his property?"

The two men relaxed. Even chuckled. "His father was Senator Hubert Grimm. The man owned half of Boston."

"I never heard of him."

"Neither had we." Hastings smiled. "But from what I hear, when Mr. Grimm arrived in New Mexico, the territorial governor practically rolled out a red carpet and kissed his feet. Within a year he'd bought this land and started constructing his house while also becoming the majority stock holder in Santa Fe's biggest bank and saloon."

"So why doesn't he live in Santa Fe if he owns so much commerce?"

"He prefers Rum River," Hastings said. "You see, while he might be a big man in Santa Fe, he couldn't own the whole town like he pretty much does Rum River."

"And I suppose," Dixie said, "the Thoroughbreds are just one of his many interests?"

The ranch hand on the other side of Dixie was in his forties, big and rugged. He dipped his chin. "Mr. Grimm has a lot of interests, but I'd have to say that horse raisin' was right at the top. Cannonade has never lost a race. And I'll eat my hat if he loses to your stallion, Miss Ballou."

"Then you'd better start soaking it in grease and gravy because I've seen Cannonade and he's just a horse. To beat High Fire, he'd have to be a winged Pegasus."

"A what?"

"It's a horse that sprang from the body of Medusa at her death."

"Who the blazes is Medusa?"

"Never mind," Dixie said, "it's Greek mythology. And don't you dare ask me what *that* is!"

The two men exchanged questioning glances and Dixie turned her attention to the ranch's impressive mansion, barns, and outbuildings coming into clear view. The mansion was obviously the focal point, a huge, white two-storied affair with a row of eight large pillars that supported an immense overhanging balcony. There were beautiful oval-topped windows and towering brick chimneys. Dixie had seen many grand Southern mansions and this one was their equal but possessed a ranch rather than a plantation flavor. Huge oaks backdropped the mansion and there were at least three acres of manicured front lawn with beds of multicolored roses. A graceful circular driveway leading up to the front porch was lined with quartz stones that glistened like diamonds.

"Ain't it something, though," Hastings said with a click of his tongue. "Miss, the first time I rode up here looking for work, I took one look at this spread and thought that I was dreaming."

"Are those the horse barns over there on the right?"

"Yep. Mr. Grimm hired some high-toned horse-raisin' people from Kentucky to design and oversee its construction. And you'll see that we have our own training and racetrack."

"Yes," Dixie said, beginning to feel overwhelmed as she followed Hastings's finger off to the left of the mansion. "I wonder why Mr. Grimm didn't suggest that we hold our race right here at this own track?"

"You'd have to ask him that yourself," Hastings said. "But most likely, it's because he don't like to have a lot of people nosing around this place. And since he figures that Rum River is his town, my guess is that he'd just as soon give the common folk like ourselves a treat. Mr. Grimm, he likes to put on his show."

"I'm sure that he does," Dixie said, watching Jack Grimm

appear on the front porch and wave, lord of all he surveyed. If there had been large cypress and magnolia trees instead of the western oak, Dixie would have sworn that she was back in the South at some rich family's Southern plantation instead of off in the wilds of the New Mexico Territory, where the Apache and mustangs still ran free.

"Miss Ballou!" Grimm called, stepping off his porch and looking devastatingly handsome in a pair of dark tailored pants, a white silk shirt, and a black bandanna loosely knotted at his throat. "Good morning!"

Dixie tried to look stern and unforgiving but it was impossible. After all, she had promised this man that she would accept his offer of employment. So how was he to know that she had changed her mind? Also, Jack Grimm couldn't be held responsible for the ungentlemanly behavior of his hired hands.

"She says she's changed her mind about working for you, Mr. Grimm!" Dick Hastings called out. "Miss Ballou said she didn't want to come but I figured you'd want to hear her tell you that in person. Right?"

Grimm's smile died. He waited until the buggy pulled up before his mansion and his burly employee had climbed down from the seat, then he extended his hand to Dixie. "I'm sure there has been some misunderstanding, Miss Ballou."

"You can say that again! I explained to these gorillas that I'd changed my mind and decided to remain in Rum River. They kidnapped me!"

"But why the change of heart, Miss Ballou?"

His distress and confusion softened her anger. "Because of the race."

When he continued to stare at her, Dixie sputtered on. "It just didn't seem like a very good idea to start working for the man who is trying to win our best Thoroughbred.

Surely you can appreciate my position."

"I'm afraid not," he replied, continuing to appear upset. "You see, after we reached an agreement yesterday, I fired the man who was in charge of my stable."

"You did?"

"Of course! That's the job I offered you. It pays . . ."

Grimm caught himself, glanced at his ranch foreman, then said, "Well, it pays quite a bit more than you might think. And anyway, the man was crude and you'd not have been able to abide by him for a single minute."

"But . . . well . . ."

"Miss Ballou. Dixie." Grimm leaned close. "Surely you can sympathize with the difficulty you've placed me in by this sudden change of heart. Out in the West, when two parties shake hands on an agreement or deal, they're expected to abide by it."

"Oh, fiddle," Dixie muttered under her breath.

"What?"

"Never mind," Dixie said with a wave of her hand. "Look, I know that my brother will want to leave as soon as this misunderstanding with the law is settled. Ruff won't remain in Rum River longer than it takes him to saddle a horse."

"He will if he wants to claim Blue Bullet for that thousand-dollar reward I'm offering. He said as much when we talked."

Grimm took Dixie's arm and slipped it through his own. "And if he loses the race, I might be willing to swap Blue Bullet for your stallion. So you see, Miss Ballou, either way, I think he'll want to go mustanging."

"You're a very persuasive man."

"How else do you think I managed to get what I have?"

Dixie decided it would be unwise to say that she knew he'd inherited his fortune. So she just smiled.

"And besides," Grimm continued, "what if I also offered your brother employment? Perhaps as my horse trainer?"

"He would turn it down cold. There are men that have to be their own boss—like you."

"But I'm also a realist. Perhaps your brother is as well. If you both stayed here for a few years, it would open up a lot of opportunities in this part of New Mexico. I might very well be able to see that you prosper and achieve even greater renown as Thoroughbred horse raisers than your father."

Dixie doubted that. "I think we're getting way ahead of ourselves."

"You're absolutely right. Why don't I show you inside my home?"

"I'd rather see your barns, paddocks, and track."

He laughed. "Of course! I should have guessed as much. And once you see the care and thought that I've put into this place, I'm sure that you'll agree it is a superb operation."

Grimm turned to his foreman. "Dick, make sure that the Ballou horses receive the finest of everything. And when Miss Ballou's luggage arrives, deposit it in that upstairs guest bedroom next to mine."

Hastings's suppressed grin spoke volumes. Dixie didn't quite know what to say and before she could think of a suitable objection, Jack was leading her off toward his horse-breeding barn.

"Now then," he said, unaware of the panicky thoughts that were racing through her mind, "did my foreman tell you anything about this stable and how I contracted some very knowledgeable Thoroughbred people from Kentucky to design it?"

"Why, yes," Dixie stammered, trying to still her raging fears. "He did."

"And wait until you see my racetrack! I've had the best footing you can imagine freighted in from Socorro. It's black, fast, and beautiful. The way some men like their women!"

He laughed. Dixie's cheeks burned.

And she wondered, What on earth have I done now?

SEVEN

"You what!" Ruff cried.

Dixie stepped back from the cell. "I realized that I couldn't go back on my word and leave Jack without a stable manager, so I agreed to stay until he found another."

Ruff shook the bars of his cell in fury. "I don't believe this! We're in the race of our lives next Sunday—where we could actually lose High Fire—and you're working for the enemy."

"He's not the enemy!" Dixie ground her teeth with exasperation. "Ruff, you're being unreasonable. This . . . this miserable cell has affected your thinking. Don't you see?"

"See what!"

"If I'm working for Jack, then I'll learn how Cannonade runs! Maybe I'll even get to ride that bay stallion."

"Fat chance. Grimm isn't stupid."

Ruff reached through the bars and gently squeezed his sister's shoulder. "Dixie, you're playing right into Jack Grimm's hands. Now, he'll be able to watch High Fire work out. And furthermore, I don't trust him."

Dixie frowned. "To do what? Forfeit Cannonade if he loses? Ruff, everyone in Rum River knows it's a match race for the horses. Even Jack couldn't welsh on the payment. I tell you, he's got the manners and chivalry of a Southern gentlemen."

"Ha!" Ruff leaned close so that the sheriff and his deputy could not overhear. "Jack Grimm is as cold-blooded as a lizard and more dangerous than a water moccasin. Have

61

you forgotten what he did to Milt's leg? What kind of a 'gentleman' could inflict that kind of suffering on another human being?"

Dixie had to concede the point. As a matter of fact, Jack had tried to visit her room the first night she'd stayed in his house but she'd locked and barricaded the inside of her door and he had gotten the message. After that, he'd minded his manners and even gone off to Rum River, probably to visit some woman.

"Dixie, that man is all wolf inside. The moment you begin to trust him, even a little, he'll use and discard you."

"Ruff, the race is Sunday. Even if we lose, Jack has agreed to talk to the judge and I'm sure he can get the charges against you dismissed. But if I quit on him now . . . well, I'm afraid that he might take it out on you. So I'm staying like I agreed. And you're just going to have to give me some credit for being able to take care of myself."

Ruff turned away, feeling bitter. He would trust Dixie with his life, but she was painfully naive. Still more girl than woman, she was no match for Jack Grimm. He'd turn her head and use her to his advantage.

"Ruff, are you all right?"

He wasn't but he steeled himself and turned, forcing a smile. "Sure. Just take care of yourself. Okay? In four or five days—certainly less than a week—I'll be out of here and we can leave Rum River maybe poorer but wiser."

"We'll win, don't you worry," Dixie vowed. "As soon as I get back to the ranch and finish exercising Jack's horses, I'll take High Fire out for a good long run. I'll do it every evening."

"Let him rest the day before the race," Ruff suggested.

"All right."

"And don't bother about visiting me until just before the race on Sunday. The important thing is to take care of yourself and the horses."

"They're living the life of luxury," Dixie said with a broad smile. "The feed is good and plentiful. Even old High Man looks like a colt the way he prances around whenever he sees one of Jack's mares. I'm sure he could give Cannonade a run for his money."

"He's never figured out that he's permanently retired," Ruff said with amusement. "But at eighteen, he'll still give High Fire a good run for the money, at least for the first half mile."

"And our mares are eating as if they were starved. You can almost see their weight coming back from one day to the next. I didn't realize how skinny our horses were until I started working at Jack's ranch. I'd guess the mares were down a hundred pounds each and the stallions close to one fifty."

"They were light," Ruff conceded, "but we've been covering a lot of ground since we left Tennessee. And they're also in the best condition of their lives."

"Well," Dixie said, "just three days to go until the race. I'll remind Jack of his promise that you are to help and oversee my race."

"Do that," Ruff said. "Tell the man that the race is off he if breaks that promise."

"I will," Dixie said. "Good-bye."

Ruff watched his sister leave. He was filled with anxiety and almost overcome with a paralyzing helplessness. More than anything, he wished he could be with Dixie to protect her from Jack Grimm who was, without a doubt, drawing her into his deceitful web. Ruff had done everything possible to warn his sister of the man's true nature, but he wasn't sure that Dixie had taken his warning to heart. She was just too damned trusting. And, in truth, she was right about the fact that, as long as she could keep Grimm at arm's length, she could at least watch and have some small influence over the wealthy rancher.

As Dixie left, Deputy Flagg entered the office. He stepped aside for Dixie and even touched the brim of his hat in greeting, but Dixie ignored him.

"Too bad, Bert," the sheriff said with a laugh. "But I'm afraid that little filly has her sights set a whole lot higher than the likes of you."

"Oh yeah?" Flagg said. "Well, little miss saucy pants is ridin' for a fall, that's for sure. Then we'll see if she don't smile at Bert and want to get cozy."

Ruff's hands clenched at his sides and when the sheriff saw his cheeks redden, he said, "Hey, Ballou, how old is your kid sister?"

Ruff glared at the man, then gave him his back.

Both Sheriff Watson and his arrogant young deputy laughed out loud. "On thing for sure," Watson heckled, "she's old enough for Mr. Grimm!"

Ruff bristled and choked down a retort that would only fuel the their gutter mentalities and give rise to even more insulting innuendos. Just hang on, Ruff told himself, the day will come when this will all change and then you can have a word in private with the sheriff and his deputy. But right now, all that Ruff could do was to say a little prayer for Dixie.

Dixie stepped down from the badly winded New Mexico Thoroughbred and handed its reins to Dick Hastings, who said, "Fast, isn't he."

"Very."

Grimm hurried over to join them. "You sure are some kind of a rider, Dixie. As skillful as a man."

"Thanks," Dixie said, knowing she was much better than most male jockeys, thanks to the fact that she had been exercising and then racing Ballou Thoroughbreds since childhood. "What do think about the track?"

"It's first class. As good as any back in Tennessee."

Jack Grimm beamed. "It ought to be! Cost me a small fortune but it's worth it. What did you think of War Cry?"

"Is that his name?" Dixie asked, biding for a moment to think out her response. She decided to tell this man and his foreman the truth. "War Cry has talent and plenty of raw speed, but he's out of condition. He shouldn't be breathing this hard and I'm sure his pulse is racing."

Grimm's smile died. "What is his pulse?"

Dixie reached up under War Cry's jaw, found a big artery, and took the young Thoroughbred's pulse. It was very high. Dixie looked at the two anxious men and said, "This horse ran a pretty good first half mile but he was flagging badly down the homestretch and his pulse is about a hundred forty beats a minute. That's much too high."

"Too high?" Hastings looked to his boss, then back to Dixie. "Why, there's nothing wrong with that!"

"I'm telling you," Dixie said, "the horse is not in anything approaching racing condition. If I were you, Mr. Grimm, I'd work him at a half mile and then build him up slowly. Otherwise, he could break down. War Cry just isn't in shape to run a fast mile."

Grimm wasn't pleased. "The trainer you replaced told me that my horses were all in excellent running shape."

"For a quarter or half mile, tops." Dixie could not help but add, "I assume that Cannonade is in a lot better condition and plenty ready to stand up against High Fire for a mile, huh?"

"Of course! You can tell he's in great shape just by looking at him. Don't get your hopes up, Dixie. Cannonade will breeze a mile. Why, I'm in the habit of galloping him all the way to Rum River without stopping and he doesn't so much as break a sweat."

"I'm sure," Dixie said, detecting unbidden doubts in the eyes of the rancher and his foreman. "But maybe you'd like me to work Cannonade, just to make sure."

Grimm threw his head back and laughed. "Ha! Not a chance! I'll work him myself this afternoon."

Dixie had a feeling that she would not be allowed to watch Cannonade's workout and she was right. That afternoon, Jack sent her into Rum River to tell Ruff that he would be allowed to attend the race as promised.

"I'm convinced that Cannonade is not in shape to run a mile," Dixie whispered through the cell bars. "I haven't seen Jack or anyone else work that stallion yet. He says he gallops him all the way from the ranch into town, but I don't believe that, either."

"But surely the man knows the condition of his own horse."

"Not necessarily. The trainer that I replaced must have been in complete charge of Jack's Thoroughbreds. And even though Jack talks a good game and seems to know a lot about bloodlines and pedigrees, he's not all that much of a horseman."

"In that case, I'm glad he's Cannonade's rider."

"We'll see," Dixie said, her voice filled with doubt. "As I was riding into town just now, I passed a small but muscular fella on his way out to the ranch. He was on a fine horse and you could tell at a glance that he was a professional jockey. I could be wrong, but I think he's the one that will actually race Cannonade. Jack is getting worried. He's seen me ride and he's seen High Fire work out. He understands that there is a very good chance he could lose his number one stallion."

"I hope you didn't work High Fire at full speed."

"No, of course not! But you know how magnificently he runs, even at half speed. That long, smooth stride of High Fire's is a thing of beauty. Jack and his foreman both watched and when I passed the quarter pole where they were standing, I could read the worry on their faces. Then, later, when I discovered that Jack's horses were sorely lacking a conditioning program, I really filled them with doubts."

"That might have been the wrong thing to do," Ruff said. "It would have been much better to have left Grimm thinking he had the race cinched. Now, he'll probably resort to some pretty desperate measures. You can bet that I'll remind him he promised to jockey his own horse on Sunday."

"I'll be very surprised if he keeps that promise," Dixie said. "I'm planning on facing that professional jockey I described."

"Is High Fire feeling good?"

"Wonderful."

"And his appetite?"

"Ravenous," Dixie assured her brother. "I took him out east of the ranch yesterday morning before anyone was up and raced him a mile and a half. He scorched the earth, so quit worrying so much!"

Ruff mustered a smile. "I will. It's just that, being locked up in this damned cell, your mind gets to playing games. Pretty soon, you start to think of all the things that could go wrong."

"Nothing will 'go wrong,' Ruff. I've got it under control. I'll feed High Fire heavy tonight and light in the morning. The race is due to start at noon and I'll come get you out of here at least an hour ahead of time. Everything has been taken care of and we are going to win tomorrow."

"I hope that Grimm wants to buy Cannonade back for a thousand dollars," Ruff said. "If we could sell him back and then go out and capture Blue Bullet . . . well, it would be a dream come true for us, Dixie. The first real break we've had since leaving Tennessee."

"It's going to happen," she promised. "Just have faith and try to get a good night's sleep. Tomorrow is going to be a great day. We're going to show Jack Grimm and all of these people how real racehorses are capable of running the mile."

"I wish the race were going to be at Grimm's track instead of through the middle of this town. At least then we wouldn't have to worry about some drunken fool stepping out in front of High Fire."

Dixie sighed. "I swear you are going to worry yourself into an early grave, Ruff! And if someone were actually drunk or stupid enough to step in front of High Fire when he was running full out, why, they'd just get trampled and we'd still win the race. I tell you, I can feel in my bones that Cannonade is going to fade badly in the last half of the race. He just doesn't have the bottom to run flat out for a mile."

"I'm sure you're right. But a lot of things can happen. You know our father's rule of racing."

"Of course I do and I don't need you to repeat it to me again," Dixie said, giving her brother's hand a squeeze and then turning to leave. "Sleep well, Ruff, we can't lose tomorrow!"

The sheriff and the deputy burst into guffaws. Ruff flushed with anger but Dixie ignored the pair as she marched outside, climbed into the saddle, and galloped away.

EIGHT

On race day, Dixie awakened shortly after daybreak and dressed quickly. She hurried downstairs then passed through the kitchen, scooping up four apples and a hunk of sourdough bread. Devouring the bread and saving the apples for her horses, Dixie rushed across the beautifully manicured yard with the rising sun casting a golden patina across the ranch and outbuildings. A rooster crowed from over near the barn and Dixie judged it was going to be a perfect day for a big horse race.

Dixie had never felt more confident that High Fire could win a race and was so optimistic she even began to sing "Dixie's Land," one of the South's most beloved songs.

> *I wish I was in the land of cotton*
> *Old times there are not forgotten*
> *Look away! Look away! Look away, Dixieland.*
> *In Dixie Land where I was born,*
> *Early on one frosty morning*
> *Look away! Look away! Look away, Dixieland.*
>
> *Then I wish I was in Dixie, hooray! Hooray!*
> *In Dixie Land, I'll take my stand*
> *To live and die in Dixie.*
> *Away, away, away down south in Dixie*
> *Away, away, away down south in Dixie!*

"Well, Miss Southern Belle," the nasal voice said, "I'm afraid that you're going to sing a different tune when you

69

see how your poor stallion took terrible sick last night."

"Away, away, away down South in—what!"

Alex, Grimm's ringer jockey who had arrived the day before, shook his muscular shoulders. "I got up early to check on the things and your racehorse was coughin' like crazy. I'm surprised that you didn't hear him all the way from the house."

The apples spilled from Dixie's cradling arms and she began to run, hearing Alex yell, "Musta et some dusty or moldy hay or something! Damn shame, Miss Ballou!"

Dixie rushed into the barn just as High Fire began to cough. It was a horrible, blasting cough, one coming from deep down in the belly. Four, five, six times it filled the barn before Dixie could reach High Fire's stall, slide the bolt, and fling the door open.

"Oh my God!" she cried. "What is wrong!"

High Fire's head was down and his eyes were heavy lidded and watering. He had the dry heaves and his belly was pumping like an accordion. After each powerful contraction, the stallion groaned and wheezed.

Dixie couldn't believe this was the same magnificent racehorse that she had seen the evening before retiring. She took High Fire's pulse and found that it was just over eighty, far too fast for a resting Thoroughbred. High Fire's breathing was rapid and when she looked into the animal's eyes, they appeared feverish and Dixie was certain that the stallion was running a temperature.

"You've been poisoned," Dixie whispered, her own heart beginning to race. "Someone has deliberately poisoned you!"

Dixie threw a halter on High Fire and had to coax the horse out of his stall. High Fire was unsteady of gait and Dixie began to weep as she led the horse outside. The smallish man she judged to be Grimm's closet jockey was gone and the yard was empty. Dixie threw back her head and yelled, "Help! Help!"

Over and over she yelled until Dick Hastings and several of the others arrived on the run, all in various stages of dress. The foreman took one glance at High Fire and said, "He don't look good, does he."

"He might die!"

"What do you want us to do?"

"Support him," Dixie said quickly. "We got to keep High Fire on his feet and moving. If he lies down, I'm afraid that he might never get up again!"

"Come on, boys! Let's help her out!"

The ranch hands pushed up against High Fire and they began to lead the stallion around. It was obvious that High Fire didn't want to walk because he kept trying to stop, and when he began to cough, his body convulsed so violently that he seemed in danger of shaking off his own feet.

"Where is Mr. Grimm!" Dixie called. "Where is that lying swindler!"

"He went to Rum River last night," Hastings said. "There's a woman . . . anyway, he said he wasn't coming back until this morning to get Cannonade. I was supposed to have him all ready by nine o'clock and we were going to lead him and this here horse into town hitched to the back of the buggy."

"Someone poisoned High Fire," Dixie wailed, tugging on the stallion's lead rope. "Look at him! He was poisoned!"

Hastings looked her square in the eye. "Well, it wasn't me that did it and it sure wasn't Mr. Grimm. As for the rest of the boys, I can't say."

"Where is that little stranger that arrived in a buggy yesterday! Alex. I'll bet he did this!"

One of the ranch hands pointed to a plume of dust vanishing into the sunrise toward Rum River. "Unless I miss my guess, there goes your man."

"Damn him!" Dixie cried in helpless fury.

They kept walking High Fire around and around the barn, the stallion coughing and Dixie crying. Someone found some elixir that was used for the colic and Dixie, in her desperation, poured the entire bottle down High Fire's throat. After an hour or so, the stallion seemed to be on the mend. It still coughed, but not as hard, and its head lifted a few degrees. But High Fire's eyes remained dull, his step heavy and hesitant.

"Here comes Mr. Grimm!" one of the men yelled. "And he's got Alex with him!"

It was true. Jack Grimm was driving his buggy hard and Alex was slumped over on the seat, apparently unconscious.

When Grimm pulled the buggy up and jumped out, he ran straight over to Dixie. He took one look at her and then he turned his attention to High Fire. "How is he?"

"He's awful!" Dixie wailed. "What did Alex use to poison this horse!"

"I have no idea! He was supposed to ride Cannonade. I pulled a muscle in my groin two days ago and knew that I wasn't up to a horse race."

Grimm frowned and lowered his eyes. "And frankly, Dixie, after seeing your horse work out on my track . . . well, I just thought it would be fairer all the way around to find a lighter rider than myself. One that matched your weight."

"So you hired that . . . that monster and he drugged my horse!"

"He wasn't supposed to! All he was asked to do was to ride Cannonade and win."

"I don't believe you!" Dixie reared back and slapped Grimm across the face so hard that his lips broke.

Grimm touched his bloody mouth. "Dammit, I told you the truth!"

"You're a bald-faced liar!"

Grimm's eyes narrowed. "You're fired, Miss Ballou! You get your horses and get off this ranch—now! And I'll see you on the starting line in"—he ripped a gold-plated pocket watch from his vest—"in exactly four hours!"

"This horse can't run!"

"Then you'll just have to forfeit him, won't you," Grimm said. "Either that or I'll sue you for breach of contract, fraud, and libel! And then I'll take all four of your Thoroughbreds! Now, get off my property!"

Dixie took another swing at the rancher's handsome face, this time hoping to blacken the rich man's eye. But Grimm caught her wrist and threw her to the ground.

Picking herself up, Dixie said, "My brother was right about you, Jack! He said you were as cold-blooded as a lizard and more dangerous than a water moccasin. But I wouldn't listen. I even argued that you were an honorable man. That you had a Southerner's code of chivalry. Ha! That just goes to show how little I know about men . . . or those who pose as men."

Grimm lifted his hand to strike her but Dick Hastings caught his wrist. "Don't do it, boss. Don't give her the satisfaction."

Grimm muttered a curse and shook his foreman away. Wheeling about, he marched toward his house yelling, "Four hours, Miss Ballou! And you had better be ready to race one mile!"

Dixie knuckled her angry tears away. "Thanks," she whispered to Hastings.

"It wasn't anything. But I'll tell you something, Miss Ballou. Jack Grimm wouldn't have played this kind of underhanded game. No siree! Not even to keep from losing Cannonade."

"Are you really so blind that you believe that?" Dixie asked with amazement.

"Yes. You see, Mr. Grimm loves horses. He might do men and even women wrong, but not horses. Whatever that little beat-up skunk in the buggy did, he did on his own."

Dixie dusted herself off. She took High Fire's lead rope and said, "Well, none of that matters now, does it? This horse won't be in any shape to run a mile. So we've lost."

"What about that old stallion? He looks to be in mighty good shape."

"He's eighteen! Cannonade is what . . . four?"

"Yes, but . . ."

"Could you outrun a fast and healthy twenty-year-old man?"

"No," Hastings admitted, "but if the stakes were high enough, I'd at least try. Now, since it looks like this stallion is going to live, we'll go get your other three Thoroughbreds and see you to the front gate. I'm sorry, but that's as much as I can allow without risking my own job. And good jobs, for a man my age, are getting damned hard to find."

The three miles into Rum River were the longest three miles of Dixie's life. She rode High Man and led poor High Fire and the brood mares. High Fire was feeling better yet was a long way from being his normal fractious and frisky self. Head down, he plodded up the road looking like an old draft horse done in after a hard day pulling a plow.

When the townspeople and those who'd come from far and wide to see what had been promoted as a great Thoroughbred race saw Dixie and her horses, they flocked around her. Dixie was assaulted with a barrage of questions concerning High Fire and finally, she pulled rein and shouted, "We've got to race or forfeit this sick stallion!

So I'm racing the horse I'm riding!"

"You're riding *this* stallion?"

"You bet I am," Dixie said, lifting her reins and High Man's head a little. "In his prime, he was never beaten and he can still run like a wild thing. And anyone can see he's in good shape."

"Yeah, for an old horse, he's a wonder," a man said sarcastically, "but he is what, ten years past his prime?"

"He's still fast and doesn't know the meaning of quit. But you go ahead and bet on Cannonade," Dixie told them. "It doesn't matter a whit to me. All I can say is that Cannonade is out of shape and Mr. Grimm isn't a shadow of the rider that I am, and he's forty pounds heavier. And that's why I figure we still have a chance."

"You're just talking hot wind!" a chubby man in a bowler yelled. "Miss, you'd be about as well off to race one of these old brood mares you're leading!"

The crowd howled with derisive laughter. It stung Dixie and made her reckless. "Just you wait and see how fast this horse is!" she challenged. "Why, only last year he outran the fastest horse in Austin."

"What kind of sorry horses do them Texans have over there, anyway!"

More laughter.

Dixie, realizing that she was just going to be mocked even worse if she tried to defend old High Man, decided to stop talking and let the old Thoroughbred do the talking for them both. And while she doubted that the valiant High Man could outrun even an out-of-shape Cannonade, it might be interesting. If she could stay within a dozen horse lengths by the half-mile mark, Dixie believed that the old stallion was in fine enough condition to overtake his much younger opponent and perhaps even steal the win at the finish line. Especially if Jack Grimm was as inexperienced a jockey as Dixie figured the rich man to be.

Dixie rode into Dobler's Livery and dismounted with the crowd still in tow. "Mr. Dobler, I know that I still owe you board money from before, but I need to put my horses up here for a few hours before the race and not worry about someone messing with them. Can I do that, sir?"

"Sure," the man said. "Put 'em back in the same stalls they was in before. You want them grained?"

"If you don't mind. We'll figure some way to pay you, I swear."

"I know that," the liveryman said, gathering reins and halter ropes. "Now, you don't worry about a thing, hear?"

"Thank you," Dixie said, starting for the sheriff's office.

Now, more than ever, Dixie needed to have Ruff by her side. Ruff would know what to do, even in a defeat that would cost them the one stallion that they'd planned to build a horse-racing dynasty upon and which represented all their hopes for the future.

NINE

Sheriff George Watson winked at Deputy Flagg and drawled, "I ain't heard nothing about our prisoner being allowed to get out of jail for no horse race, have you, Bert?"

Bert smirked at Dixie. "Nope. Seem to me it'd be highly unusual. After all, we don't let prisoners go to church or Sunday school, either, do we?"

Watson chortled, fat belly rippling with mirth. "No siree! And I never let prisoners go to no travelin' tent revivals, either!"

Dixie stomped her boot down hard. "All right, you've both had your laughs! But you'll be laughing out your backsides when Mr. Grimm finds out that you won't release Ruff for the race. That was his promise."

"He ain't told us nothing about no release," Watson said, managing to stop laughing. "And from what I heard, he's booted you off'n his place. Probably had his fill of you real quick and—"

"That'll be enough!"

Everyone turned to see Jack Grimm standing in the doorway. His lips were swollen and he looked furious as he stomped into the office. Pinning Watson with his eyes, he said, "Sheriff, your days in this office are numbered. Now let the prisoner out for this damned race before I put you inside that cell instead."

"But, Mr. Grimm! I thought . . ."

"As usual, you thought wrong." Grimm marched past

Dixie, and when he reached the sheriff's desk, he stuck out his hand, palm upward. "Give me the damned key, George!"

Sheriff Watson found the key in a hurry. "I'll do it! I'll do it!" he fretted, scurrying across the office.

Ruff waited until the key turned and then he kicked the door hard. It banged into the sheriff, causing him to curse. "Damn you! You'll pay for that!"

"Not as much as you're going to pay for keeping me locked up in here," Ruff warned, marching over to stand beside his sister.

"Ruff," she said, "someone poisoned High Fire. He'll recover, but he's not able to run."

"Then the race is off this weekend," Ruff said. "We can either have it later, or just forget the whole damned thing and head for Santa Fe."

"You're not going to do either," Grimm announced. "Rum River is bursting with folks that came down from Santa Fe and the surrounding country to see a horse race, and that's just what is going to take place."

"You expect us to enter a sick horse!"

"No," Dixie interrupted, holding Ruff back. "He expects us to race High Man."

"High Man is eighteen years old!"

Grimm shrugged his shoulders. "We've a deal, Ballou. We made a race and it's not my problem if your horse is sick. I am, however, willing to allow the substitution because so many people have arrived in this town expecting a horse race."

"You are just a real saint, aren't you," Ruff said cryptically. "Doesn't take any nerve to race a young horse against an old one. I expect no one else is going to be very impressed. In fact, you're going to wind up the laughingstock on the territory."

Grimm took a frowning backstep. "I don't much care what people say about me. I'll have your Thoroughbred and you'll be facing a judge that I can influence. So what else matters?"

"Your reputation, what little you might still have," Dixie said. "Everyone will know what happened to our racehorse the morning of the race. No one will mark it up as a simple coincidence."

Grimm glanced at the sheriff and then the deputy. He turned and walked over to the doorway, then he pivoted around and said, "All right, maybe I'll even the odds a little and give you a five-second head start on that old stallion."

"Five seconds!" Dixie's laugh was cold. "That's a joke and we both know it. Fifteen seconds at least."

Ruff held his breath until Grimm finally said, "All right. Fifteen seconds. Ruff, I'll even let you be the timer. But not a second more!"

Ruff tried to hide his excitement and he avoided looking at Dixie when he said, "How's the race going to be laid out?"

"It's real simple," Grimm replied. "Dixie and I will trot out the east end of Rum River for a mile. You can be the starter but you'll be right here at the finish line," he said, pointing into the street.

"How's that going to work?"

"Simple," Grimm said. "You start your sister with a rifle shot right outside the sheriff's door. We'll both hear it plain. Fifteen seconds later, fire a second shot and I'll start Cannonade."

"But, Mr. Grimm!" the sheriff protested. "We can't let this man have a rifle!"

"He's right, Mr. Grimm," the deputy said. "Why don't you let me fire the shots?"

Grimm thought it over and finally nodded with acceptance. "All right."

Ruff pulled Dixie over to one corner of the office and they went into a huddle, trying to keep their voices from being overheard.

"We've got a good chance to win this," Dixie told her brother "Cannonade is a few pounds overweight and I'm betting he's out of shape."

"Then ride out just as far as he'll allow," Ruff said. "We want the race as long as possible. And we also want that fifteen-second lead to stretch out as long as possible."

"I'll do what I can," Dixie promised. "And High Fire is going to be all right," Dixie added with assurance. "He was coughing and wheezing real bad but now he's much better. It's just that he's still weak."

"Any idea who did it?"

"Yes. But the man has already suffered. Mr. Grimm caught up with and beat him silly."

"He took a right good shot in the mouth doing it," Ruff said, remembering Grimm's broken lips.

"No, I hit him in the mouth."

"Oh."

"I shouldn't have done it," Dixie admitted. "But I was furious."

"You had every right to be. I'll bet he gave the order to have High Fire poisoned."

"That's what I thought at first, but not anymore. Mr. Hastings, his foreman, has been nice to me and I believed him when he told me that Jack Grimm thinks too much of good horses to allow that kind of an underhanded thing to occur."

Ruff wasn't sure if he believed that or not. All he knew for sure was that Jack Grimm was insisting on a horse race today instead of acting like a gentleman and postponing the race until High Fire was fit again.

"All right, Miss Ballou, let's go!" Grimm called, sticking his head back into the office.

Before she pulled away to follow the rancher, Ruff said, "Just don't worry about a thing except winning the race, Dixie."

"But what if I *don't* win! Then we lose High Fire and you're still in jail and . . ."

"It'll work out," Ruff said. "Either way, this is going to work out."

"I wish I had your confidence," Dixie said. "But I don't. I keep thinking that maybe poor old High Man might rupture something inside or break a leg or . . ."

"Stop it!" Ruff lowered his voice. "High Man has been raced hundreds of times and that old horse knows what to do. Just give him his head and let him run at his own pace. And when you come racing into town, don't let anything or anyone stop you from crossing the finish line. Hear me?"

"Yes."

"I'll do what I can at this end. Together, we'll win this race and once we have Cannonade, we're going to have some chips to start bargaining with. Just you wait and see, Dixie."

Dixie knew what Ruff was trying to say. If they won the race, there would be so many people that even Jack Grimm could not welsh on the bet. He'd have to forfeit his best Thoroughbred and he'd want Cannonade back in the worst way possible. That being the case, a deal could be struck and Ruff would be free again, perhaps even with some bounty in the exchange.

There was an immense crowd outside the sheriff's office and they were deluging Jack Grimm with anxious questions. Grimm reached out for Dixie's hand and nearly pulled her off her feet. A few moments later, they were climbing onto the back of a buckboard and Grimm was holding up his hands and yelling to the crowd for silence.

"Everyone, please listen!" he called. "I know that you're all upset about this new match, but let me tell you, it's still a hell of a gamble on my part."

The crowd booed and jeered.

"Listen!" Grimm yelled. "I'm giving Miss Ballou a fifteen-second head start! And her horse, despite its age, has never been beaten!"

"This century or last!" a heckler shouted.

"Dammit, Dixie, make a case for your horse or this bet is off!" Grimm hissed. "If that happens, I'll make sure that your brother goes to the territorial prison and he'll be an old man before he's set free. I mean it!"

Dixie knew that Jack Grimm wasn't bluffing. He had his own code of ethics but he was also a man to whom pride was second only to money. And right now, pride was taking an awful beating.

"Everyone, listen to me!" Dixie called. "What Mr. Grimm has just told you is true! High Man has never lost a race and he's sound and still very, very fast! If you don't believe me, clear the street. I'll go get my horse and show you what he can do!"

Before Grimm could stop her, Dixie jumped down and ran over to the stable. In a few minutes, she emerged from Dobler's Livery and she let High Man lay back his ears and run. The old stallion responded to the drum of Dixie's heels with a burst of speed that send him flying down main street with people scattering like a covey of quail in order to keep from getting run over.

At the west end of town, Dixie wheeled High Man around and came flying back. When she neared the sheriff's office, she reined the old stallion in and surveyed the sea of stunned faces.

"This is a Ballou stallion!" she proclaimed. "And you can see that he's fit and can still outrun most anything on four legs in this part of the country."

"And you're giving her a *fifteen-second head start*?" a man asked, breaking the silence and looking at Jack Grimm as if he were daft.

"That's right," Grimm said, appearing shocked to realize how fast High Man really was despite his age.

The crowd gazed with wonderment at Dixie and her stallion until someone wagered ten dollars on High Man to win, then the betting started with a frenzy.

Grimm jumped down from the buckboard and went over to the deputy. Dixie could almost guarantee that he was instructing the deputy to shorten the fifteen-second interval between the two starts. Her eyes locked with Ruff's eyes and a clear understanding passed between them—Ruff must delay the deputy's second shot.

As they rode out to the east end of town on their two stallions, Dixie tried to contain her excitement but obviously failed because High Man began to nervously prance and so did Cannonade.

"They know," Grimm said. "Somehow, they know."

"They can feel our tension through the stirrup leathers and through the reins," Dixie explained. "And you're going to have a hard time holding your stallion in when High Man takes off running."

"I'll turn him facing away," Grimm said, looking worried but determined.

"Are you going to be all right? No sense in risking your life to win a race."

"I'll be fine!" Grimm snapped. "I can handle this stallion. Just try and keep yourself from getting killed or running someone down."

"The only way that anyone will get run down by my

horse is if they're stupid enough to try and stop us from
crossing that finish line ahead of you."

"I think we've gone a mile now," Grimm said.

Dixie acted as if she didn't hear the man. She just kept
riding and Cannonade was giving Grimm such a fit that he
had no choice but to follow along. Each yard farther out
from town would work in High Man's favor.

"I said we've gone a mile!" Grimm shouted. "This is far
enough."

"Not quite," Dixie countered. "We need to ride at least
another hundred yards."

"By gawd we've gone at least a mile!"

Dixie kept riding until, finally, Grimm managed to rein
in Cannonade. "This is as far as I'm going! If you want to
start farther out, that's your choice. But you're still only
getting fifteen seconds' head start."

Dixie could see that it served no good purpose to keep
riding. She reined High Man up and then rode back to
Grimm and waved her hand at Rum River as a signal that
they were in position and ready to start the race.

Back in town, the crowd's excitement was contagious. It
always had been and now, despite the desperation of their
circumstances, Ruff felt confident that Dixie and High Man
would somehow manage to win this crucial race. He stood
in front of the sheriff's office with Watson at one elbow
and the rifle-toting deputy at the other.

"They're ready!" a keen-eyed observer shouted from the
middle of the otherwise deserted street.

"Here goes, then," Deputy Flagg said, raising his rifle
into the sky and firing it.

"The girl is off!" the observer shouted, dashing to the
side of the street lined by spectators.

Deputy Flagg handed his rifle to a man who held a second

single-shot rifle. Cocking the weapon, he raised it, but Ruff batted the weapon down. "Wait fifteen seconds!"

Flagg cursed and drove the rifle's butt at Ruff's face. Ruff dodged the blow and booted Flagg in the shin. The deputy roared with pain and would have shot Ruff if he hadn't grabbed the rifle barrel and wrestled it skyward. The rifle exploded into the sky at the same instant that lights blossomed behind Ruff's eyes. He dropped to his knees knowing that Sheriff Watson had pistol-whipped him from behind.

Struggling to retain his senses, Ruff crawled between two men and snaked up to the street. He turned his head and now he could see Dixie and High Man flying in the lead with Cannonade on their heels.

Ruff grinned. It was hard to judge Dixie's lead from looking nearly straight on but from what he could see, High Man had a substantial lead, which Cannonade was barely eating into. Dixie was riding bent over their old Thoroughbred's withers, her hands wrapped in High Man's golden mane. In sharp contrast, Jack Grimm was leaning back in his saddle and riding loose, not helping his prized Thoroughbred at all.

"Come on!" Ruff shouted, his voice merging with that of the cheering crowd. "Come on home!"

Dixie risked a quick glance back over her shoulder when she was yet two hundred yards from the edge of Rum River. She could see that Cannonade had fire in his eyes and was flying across the ground. The New Mexico Thoroughbred had the heart of a lion but his rider was a grave handicap. Dixie smiled and let High Man come streaking into town, mane and tail flying. It was not even going to be close!

She was getting ready to sit up straight and pull on the reins when, suddenly, two men jumped out into her path, six-guns blazing skyward. Their intention was clearly to spook the old stallion, but High Man wasn't buying into their cheating game. The Ballou stallion swept past them as if they didn't even exist and when he crossed the finish line the crowd roared with delight. It seemed like a long time before Cannonade sailed across the line but it probably was not more than fifteen seconds.

Dixie was mobbed as the crowd surged around High Man. Laughing and shouting, she let them take her stallion's reins and lead High Man back up the street.

"You won," Grimm said bitterly, dismounting his gasping Thoroughbred. "You and your brother suckered me into that fifteen-second head start. I would have beaten you in an even-start race!"

"High Fire would have left you both in his dust," Dixie said, taking Cannonade's reins. "You deserved to lose."

"We'll talk later," Grimm said, making it sound more like a threat than a promise.

Dixie dismounted and when she saw her brother being yanked to his feet with blood running down from a scalp wound, she threw herself at Sheriff Watson, clawing for his eyes. He probably would have pistol-whipped her, too, only there were too many witnesses. Instead, Deputy Flagg grabbed and shoved her aside.

A moment later, Ruff, half dragged and half prodded, was thrown back into his cell.

Taking up the reins to both stallions, Dixie vowed that she would not wait for Jack Grimm to find and talk to her—she would strike a deal with the man within the hour. And if that meant trading Cannonade for her brother's freedom, she'd gladly do so.

TEN

Jack Grimm was in no mood for the crowds of horse race bettors that would pack Rum River's saloons. The jubilant winners would gloat over his defeat and forfeit of Cannonade, while the much larger crowd of losing bettors would be surly and even combative. What would happen, Grimm knew, was that he would lose his temper and get into a brawl. And while he was not afraid of a fight, his lips were already broken and he'd had enough trouble packed into this rotten day.

"Where are you going?" Dick Hastings called.

"Over to see Tina. Don't expect to see me back at the ranch for a day or even two."

Hastings nodded with understanding. Tina was Grimm's lady friend. A tall, brassy gal with auburn hair and a fierce streak of independence, she worked in one of the saloons and sometimes entertained a few "special" and well-heeled friends like Jack Grimm. It was said that Tina had once been a singer and dancer on California's infamous Barbary Coast, a rival of the famed Spider Dancer, Miss Lola Montez. Hastings didn't know about that, but he had heard Tina sing and she had a talent that matched her exceptional good looks.

Jack watched his boss disappear into the saloon where Tina worked, then he headed for a saloon of his own with a powerful thirst building in his throat. Once inside, he wasted no time in shouldering his way to the bar. "Whiskey!" he commanded.

"Comin' right up!"

"Leave the bottle, Mitch. I'm going to tie one on in the next few hours."

"Whatever you say," the bartender replied, rushing off to serve the other boisterous patrons.

Hastings was not normally much of a drinker but watching Cannonade getting decisively beaten by an eighteen-year-old Tennessee horse was damned upsetting. Furthermore, Hastings knew that life at the ranch was going to be tense working under a humiliated Jack Grimm. Grimm would take the loss personally and the forfeit of their number one stallion was a blow to the entire outfit.

An hour later, Dick Hastings was starting to feel better about life and getting the loss of Cannonade in perspective when the man next to him at the bar turned and growled, "Hey, girls ain't allowed in here!"

Hastings turned to see a visibly upset Dixie glaring at him. "Best go, Miss Ballou. Like the man says, this isn't any place for a girl."

"Where is Mr. Grimm?"

"He's busy. You got his prized stallion, now leave him alone."

"I don't give a damn about Cannonade. I want my brother!"

"Sorry," Hastings said. "But I'm not the sheriff or the judge. Talk to them."

Dixie grabbed his arm. "You have to take me to Mr. Grimm. I'll trade his stallion back for my brother's freedom."

Hastings tossed down another shot of whiskey. "That's a thousand-dollar horse you're talking about, Miss Ballou. You sure that brother of yours is worth so much money? Why, the most prison time he could get is a year or two."

"Please," Dixie begged. "The sheriff pistol-whipped Ruff and then he and his deputy dragged him inside. God only

knows what they might be planning next. Ruff might already
be dead! If you're really a decent and honorable man, you've
got to help me!"

Hastings saw the tears and heard the desperation in
Dixie's voice. "Mitch," he called, slapping a dollar on the
bar, "save me the bottle for later!"

"Yes, sir!"

"Come on," Hastings said, leading Dixie outside. "I think
the first thing we'd better do is to look in on your big
brother."

"I've searched all over town for Mr. Grimm. I can't find
him anywhere and no one will tell me where he's gone!"

"I think I can find him for you," Hastings said with
assurance as he took her arm. "But first, let's check in
on your brother to make sure that there aren't any fatal
'accidents' taking place before we can get things straightened out between you and Mr. Grimm."

"Thank you!"

When they marched into the sheriff's office, Watson was
nowhere to be seen and Deputy Flagg was standing beside
the cell rubbing his bruised knuckles.

One look at her battered brother sent Dixie into a rage.

"You've beat him!" she cried, attacking the deputy.

This time, Flagg was ready. He ducked under Dixie's fist
and grabbed her around the waist. "Woop-ee!" he called,
whirling Dixie around in a complete circle while laughing
like a hyena.

"All right!" Hastings shouted, drawing and aiming his
six-gun in the deputy's general direction. "Put Miss Ballou
down nice and easy."

The laughter died in Flagg's eyes. He dumped Dixie to
the floor and glared at Hastings. "Don't you think you're
out of line, pullin' a gun on a deputy like that?"

"No, I sure as hell don't," Hasting said, looking past

Dixie to Ruff. "I can see that you're up to your usual viciousness. Must take a hell of a lot of courage to beat a man that's already unconscious, huh, Bert?"

"Shut up!"

Hastings cocked back the hammer of his six-gun. "I could do this whole town a big favor by drilling you cold. I could say that you were about to murder your prisoner and when I tried to stop you, you went for your gun."

"Who'd believe that! Dick, you're talking crazy! What's wrong with you!"

"I hate cowards and bullies," Hastings drawled. "I always have and probably always will. That being the case, I'm afraid this town isn't big enough for the both of us. That means you're going to get on your horse and skedaddle. And if I ever see you in Rum River again, I'll shoot you on sight. Same as I would a rabid dog."

The deputy's mouth opened to protest but when the ranch foreman raised his Colt and took aim, Flagg's nerve broke. "All right! All right! I'm leaving! Don't shoot!"

Dixie snatched up a set of keys from the sheriff's desk and rushed to open the cell. Once inside, she began to minister to her unconscious brother.

It was only a few minutes before Sheriff Watson rushed into his office, and demanded, "What's the meaning of this!"

"Your deputy used this girl's brother as a punching bag. I told him I'd shoot him on sight. That's about the long and short of it, Watson."

"You can't do that!"

"I did it." Hastings turned to face the sheriff. "And if you get smart with me, I'll slap you up to a peak and knock the peak off. I mean it, I'd just as soon whip as look at you, Watson."

The sheriff paled. "I . . . I'm going to speak to Mr. Grimm

about you! I'll demand that you be fired!"

"Do what you want," Hastings said, "but get out of here before I lose what's left of my patience."

Sheriff Watson blustered but he left on the run. A few minutes later, Ruff was propped up on his bunk and Dixie was wiping his battered face with a wet rag.

"Let's get him out of here," Hastings said, helping Ruff to his feet. "We'll take him over to Dobler's Livery and then we'd better square things with Mr. Grimm."

"You're really sticking your neck out," Dixie said. "I'll never forget this, and neither will Ruff."

Dick Hastings blushed. "I've done some things I'm not very proud of when I was young. Now I'm too old not to know the difference between right and wrong. Let's go."

They got Ruff over to the livery and then headed back uptown. When Hastings led her into the saloon, Dixie didn't think much about it one way or the other. But when he escorted her up the stairs and heard the catcalls, she grew uneasy.

Stopping at the top of the landing, Dixie said, "Dick, why on earth are we going up here?"

"You wanted to strike a deal with Mr. Grimm, didn't you?" the ranch foreman said, knuckles poised to knock on the door.

"Yes, but . . ."

"Well, this is where he'll be for the next two or three days. You're old enough to guess what he's doing."

Dixie felt her cheeks warm. "We can't . . ."

Hastings shrugged his broad shoulders. "It's up to you, Miss. If you want to play the innocent Southern belle, we can leave. In a few days, Mr. Grimm will probably show his face and—"

"No," Dixie said, squaring her shoulders. "We can't wait a few days. I want to get this settled right now."

"Okay, then," Hastings said, "but this might not be much fun."

"Knock," Dixie ordered.

Hastings knocked on the door. There was no answer. He knocked harder.

"Go away!" a woman's strident voice demanded. "I'm busy!"

"Miss Tina, it's Dick Hastings. I got to talk to Mr. Grimm."

"Go away!"

But Hastings wasn't of a mind to go away. He pounded on the door even harder. Both he and Dixie heard muffled curses as someone marched to the door.

"Best stand back," Hastings warned, retreating all the way across the hall. "Tina has an Irish temper and she's going to be spittin' like a wet cat."

Dixie retreated and when the door flew open, she even pressed her back against the wall. Tina was nearly six feet tall, with a wild shock of red hair and thick makeup. She was wearing nothing but a sheet and that was none too carefully wrapped around her voluptuous body. Dixie was glad that the hallway was dim because she knew her cheeks were flaming.

"Dick, I'm going to . . . who the hell is that!"

"Her name is Miss Dixie Ballou. She's got to talk to Mr. Grimm."

"Among other things, he's getting drunk," Tina snapped. "And you're both gettin' lost."

Tina started to slam the door shut between them but Dick Hastings threw his foot in the way, then yelled, "Boss! Dixie wants to trade you Cannonade back for her brother. Deputy Flagg damned near beat him to death in his cell awhile ago."

Tina's fists balled at her sides. "Dick, if you don't get

your damned foot outta my door, I'll bite it off at the ankle!"

"Come on, Tina! Can't you see that the girl is just tryin' to save her brother's life? Cut her a little slack."

"Let 'em in," Grimm called. "What the hell, we might as well make this a party."

Dixie didn't wait for a second invitation. Mustering all of her determination, she pushed past the Amazon woman and hurried inside to see a half-dressed, half-drunk Jack Grimm sprawled across an enormous bed with a green satin bedspread.

"So," Grimm said, raising a glass of whiskey. "You want to trade me Cannonade for your brother."

"That's right."

"I don't want him anymore."

"Cannonade? Or my brother?"

"Cannonade! He lost the damned race to an old horse! What would I want with a loser?"

Dixie had not been prepared for this surprise. "Well, sir," she stammered, trying to form an argument. "High Man may be old, but he's still deceptively fast. And he was carrying fifty or sixty pounds less than Cannonade. Don't blame your horse because we had too much a head start and you can't ride near as well as I can."

"What?"

Realizing her mistake, Dixie quickly added, "Well, I'm like my brothers. A horseman. A horsewoman, really. But what I'm trying to say is that I've been exercising Thoroughbreds on the track since I was ten years old. And I've been racing them for my family since I was thirteen. You can't expect to know as much as I do about racehorses, Mr. Grimm."

"I know a hell of a lot about Thoroughbreds!"

"Oh sure, about their bloodlines. But you don't really understand them. Me and my family have a gift, Mr. Grimm. But so do you!"

"Oh yeah, and what exactly do you think is my 'gift'?"

"Making money, of course! Why, my family did all right back in Tennessee before we lost everything because of the war. But we never had anywhere near your kind of money or power. You're far more successful than we ever could have expected to be."

"Is that right?" Grimm asked, making no pretense of hiding his pleasure.

"It is," Dixie said, taking hope as she could see the anger draining out of the rancher. "Why, you're probably the richest and most successful man in this part of New Mexico."

Grimm nodded and sipped his drink. "Yes, I am."

"She's buryin' you with horse manure!" Tina said scornfully. "Jack, don't you let her twist you around that way! She tricked you into losing a horse race, now she wants to trick you again and you're swallowing her bull, hook, line, and sinker."

"Aw shut up, Tina," Grimm growled. "It's a straight trade. What do I care if her brother goes to prison?"

"But you just said that you didn't want a loser horse!" Tina exclaimed.

"Yeah, I know. I know. But maybe I'm really not quite the rider that Miss Ballou is. And I sure am a lot heavier. Besides, I'd want to sweeten the deal."

Tina smiled. Dixie blinked. "What do you mean? I'm offering you a horse you said is worth a thousand dollars."

"*Was* worth a thousand dollars," Grimm corrected. "What kind of stud fees do you think I'll get now that Cannonade has lost to an old horse—even one with a lighter, better rider and a fifteen-second head start?"

"Well . . ."

"His stud fee will be half what it was before the race," Grimm continued. "And what about all his offspring that I'm raising? Do you suppose that *their* value might also be worth about ten cents on the dollar after today's fiasco?"

Dixie supposed that they might.

"So you see," Grimm said, taking another sip of his drink, "today I lost far, far more than Cannonade. I lost the value of my entire stable of Thoroughbreds."

"I'm sorry," Dixie said. "But a horse race is a horse race. You can't win them all."

Grimm licked his swollen lips. "To be perfectly honest with you, young lady, I admire your brother for stepping in and putting a halt to Milt and Pete shooting mustangs. But, on the other hand, I wish that I had never heard the name Ballou. Things were a lot better before you and your brother arrived in Rum River."

"I wish that I could help you out," Dixie said, "but . . ."

"You can help me out," Grimm interrupted. "We can race again and the next time, you'll figure out a way to lose on your young stallion, High Fire."

Dixie stared at the man. "You mean throw the race?"

"That's exactly what I mean."

"We can't do that!"

Grimm drained his glass. "Fine. Then you keep Cannonade—he's lost his value to me—and I'll make sure that your brother goes to trial, and then to prison."

When Dixie looked to Hastings for help, the foreman said, "Boss, her brother was so beat up we took him over to Dobler's Livery. He's going to need some medical attention."

"Fine. But he's under arrest and he can get it in his cell."

"And," Hastings said, "I sort of put the fear into Deputy

Flagg and run him out of town. I guess I also spooked the sheriff."

"Good! You take his place until the next election."

"I'm no lawman!"

"Neither was Sheriff Watson or his deputy. You're sheriff now, Dick. Either that, or you can pack your bags."

Hastings looked so miserable that Dixie felt sorry for the former ranch foreman. "You'll do just fine," she assured. "In fact, I think you'll make a wonderful sheriff."

"Aw, dammit! I got a lot of friends in this town. I don't want to have to throw them in jail for getting drunk and raising a little hell."

"They'll forgive you," Tina said, actually appearing sympathetic. "And the election isn't that far off."

Grimm climbed off the bed and went over to his coat hanging over the back of a chair. He selected a cigar, bit off its tip, and lit it.

Puffing, he said, "Well, Miss Ballou, have we got a deal or not? It's entirely up to you."

Dixie knew when she was whipped. And even though she didn't know how she was going to make her brother see fit to enter their young stallion in a race they were not allowed to win, she would face that when the time came and he was free again.

"It's a deal, Mr. Grimm."

"Good!"

"But High Fire won't be fit to run for a week or two at least."

"That's fine."

"And," Dixie said, "we're dead broke. I haven't the money to pay our own board bill, let alone Cannonade's added expenses."

"I'll settle accounts with Dobler for all your horses." Grimm was looking alert now and he began to pace the floor with growing excitement. "What about Blue Bullet?"

"What about him?"

"I want him!"

Dixie shrugged her shoulders. "So?"

"So if you and your brother are so great with horses, catch him for me. Catch him using Cannonade and High Man."

Dixie's eyes flashed with anger. "Is that part of the deal, too?"

"No," Grimm said. "If you catch that blue mustang stallion, the offer of one thousand dollars stands."

"I'll speak to my brother about it."

"Good! Excellent! And whatever you need in the way of provisions, rope, corral posts, or whatever, you've got them and they're on me at Robby's Mercantile."

"You take care of everything, don't you," Dixie snapped. "You use your money and your power to run all our lives. The sheriff's, your foreman's, mine, Ruff's—even the judge is under your thumb!"

"That's the golden rule," Grimm said brightly.

"What?"

"Whoever has the gold makes the rules."

Grimm laughed devilishly over his perversion of the golden rule, causing Dixie to grind her teeth with exasperation. The sooner she got back to Ruff and away from this man and his brassy, painted lady, the better.

ELEVEN

Ruff finished feeding the ailing High Fire a warm mash of oats, molasses, and some Tennessee medicinal powders that had served his father well doctoring Thoroughbreds through the years.

"How is he?" Dixie asked with concern.

"He's coming out of it, but a lot slower than I'd hoped. Did Jack Grimm ever find out how that man poisoned High Fire?"

"No. He wouldn't admit to anything. And since there was no evidence, Grimm sent him packing. He looked worse than you, Ruff. Jack just beat the hell out of him."

"That gives me small comfort," Ruff said dryly. "And if I could have gotten my hands on him, I'd . . . oh, hell! It's done."

"That's right," Dixie said. "What we have to do now is to try and trap Blue Bullet."

"That's going to be a tall order," Ruff said. "We don't know a thing about his habits. Where he waters, feeds, beds his mares down. We don't know anything."

"That's why I asked around town and found out what I could about that stallion. He's been hunted so long that I decided we'd have no chance at all of catching him without some local expertise."

Ruff cocked an eyebrow. "Like who, exactly?"

"There's an Indian named Johnny Starving Bear," Dixie said. "Dick Hastings tells me that he knows more about mustangs and this country than anyone around. But he's a little crazy."

"What does that mean?"

Dixie shrugged. "It means that he's unpredictable, fiercely independent, talks to himself, and has been known to laugh at the oddest moments."

"He sounds like bad news."

"Dick says that Johnny Starving Bear is the only man alive that understands Blue Bullet and knows that stallion's daily routine."

"If he knows so much about Blue Bullet, why hasn't Johnny Starving Bear trapped the horse himself and claimed the thousand-dollar reward?"

"Maybe he doesn't need the money? Hell, Ruff, I don't know. We'll have to ask the man to find out."

Ruff wasn't a bit excited about tying in with a crazy, laughing Indian. Mustanging was a hard, dangerous business and a man needed all his wits and stamina. To hire someone untrustworthy was just asking for trouble.

"Please, Ruff. Johnny Starving Bear lives just a few miles north of town. I've got directions and Dick assured me that Starving Bear is harmless. He said we might actually find him . . . interesting."

"Interesting, huh?"

"We need someone who knows Blue Bullet's pattern," Dixie argued. "Otherwise, we might as well let Cannonade beat High Fire as soon as he's healthy, cut our losses, and leave this town in our dust."

Ruff was feeling sore and beat to hell when he mounted Cannonade. The bay stallion began to prance and toss its head. It laid back its ears, squealed, and pawed at High Man before trying to sink its teeth in the old stallion's neck. Ruff banged his heels into Cannonade's ribs and told the animal that he was not of a mind to put up with any nonsense. The New Mexico Thoroughbred quit its foolishness, though it was clear he did not like High Man and was spoiling for a fight.

The ride out to Johnny Starving Bear's place was closer to five miles rather than two or three. Ruff was irritable and his head pounded. He made a secret vow to someday find ex-Deputy Flagg and repay the man with a beating for a beating.

"Just try and be sociable," Dixie advised, glancing sideways at her brother. "We really need this Starving Bear's help."

"Not if he's a liability."

"Just give him a chance. And since you're so set against this idea, why don't you just let me do all the talking?"

"Suits me," Ruff grumped.

Johnny Starving Bear's place was at the far end of a brush-clogged canyon bordered by high red cliffs. When they neared the end of the canyon they saw a wickiup of branches, boards, and burlap sacking.

"Nice place," Ruff said sarcastically.

"Sssh!"

Dixie would have said more except a pack of thin but ferocious dogs came boiling out from behind the wickiup. When High Man and Cannonade saw the dogs, they laid their ears back and tried to attack. It was all that Dixie and Ruff could do to control their horses, and before the fracas was over, Cannonade had managed to kick one of the snarling hounds. High Man bit another.

"Hey!" Ruff yelled at the wickiup. "Call your damned mongrels off! We come as friends!"

Dixie quirted a particularly aggressive dog across the snout and didn't even consider dismounting. "Johnny Starving Bear! Are you here! We come as friends of Dick Hastings! We want to talk to you!"

Ruff heard Cannonade grunt with pain as a big black

cur sank its fangs into the Thoroughbred's hock. The horse kicked and the cur howled in pain as it rolled over and over before shooting off into the rocks with its tail between its legs.

"They're acting like a pack of starving wolves!" Ruff shouted. "Let's get out of here!"

But just as they were about to wheel and race their Thoroughbreds back out of the canyon, a tall, skinny Indian appeared on a granite boulder above them. His expression was wild and he danced, waving a reata in one hand and a knife in the other.

Ruff's hand covered his six-gun. "Are you Johnny Starving Bear!"

"That's me, White Eyes!" the Indian yelled down at them.

"Well, how about calling off these damned dogs!"

The Indian looped his reata around his neck, jammed his knife into his waistband, and placed his thumbs under his front teeth. His whistle filled the canyon and sent the dogs racing back around the wickiup.

Ruff dismounted to examine Cannonade's hock. There was a spot of blood but, otherwise, it looked to be all right. He was furious when he glanced up at the Indian. "What kind of a reception is that! We came here to talk, not be attacked by a pack of dogs!"

Johnny Starving Bear shrugged his bare and bony shoulders as if he had no control over the situation. He looked at Dixie and when he smiled, it was without front teeth. The Indian was shirtless and you could count his every rib. He wore a breechcloth and knee-high leather moccasins. He was hatless but a thick red-and-white-checkered bandanna was wrapped around his head and his hair was long and chopped off at shoulder length.

"You're Apache, aren't you?" Dixie asked.

"Mescalero. What you want, pretty white girl?"

"Hey! Watch your manners!" Ruff warned. "She's my sister."

"Pretty anyway. What you want?"

"Can we talk a little?" Dixie asked. "It's kind of hard to carry on a conversation when you are way up there and we're way down here."

Johnny Starving Bear reminded Ruff of a famished egret or stork. Long legged, he tipped his head one way and then the other, like a tall bird looking down at an unfamiliar bug that it might spear with its beak. Finally, the Apache decided that he would talk. He vanished only to reappear a few minutes later at their sides.

"What you want?" he asked Dixie.

"Dick Hastings said that you know more about the mustangs in this country than any man alive. We intend to catch Blue Bullet. Our stallions are a match for his speed and we'll pay you well for helping us."

The Indian passively regarded Dixie. His eyes and expression gave no clue whatsoever as to his thoughts. Johnny Starving Bear just stared. First at Dixie, then at Ruff, and finally at High Man. Apparently, he had already seen and judged Cannonade.

"How much?"

"A hundred dollars," Ruff answered.

"Five hundred."

"That's ridiculous!" Ruff snapped. "The entire reward is only one thousand."

"Indians get short end of stick too long. Five hundred."

Ruff groaned. "Listen, we'll go a third. Equal partners. That's as good as we'll offer."

"Okay," the Indian grunted after long consideration.

"But only if we capture Blue Bullet and get paid by Mr. Grimm," Dixie said, making it clear that they would not pay Johnny Starving Bear unless they actually received the reward.

"How do you plan to catch that stallion when everyone else has failed?" Ruff asked the Apache with a good deal of suspicion.

"Catch him from tree."

Ruff's eyebrows shot up. "What are you talking about? You're not thinking of trying to drop on that stallion's back from a limb, are you?"

"You see."

Ruff rolled his eyes to the sky. "Dixie, I don't like this," he complained under his breath. "Seems to me that . . ."

"Shhh!" Dixie forced a smile. "What will we do, Johnny Starving Bear?"

"Lasso mares. You rope?"

"No," Ruff admitted. "Back in Tennessee where we come from, roping wasn't very popular. We just herded our horses, sheep or cattle from pasture to pasture."

Johnny Starving Bear giggled.

"Something funny about that?" Ruff challenged.

"Leave him alone!" Dixie ordered. "If he thinks that seems funny, then what's the harm."

Ruff did not like or trust the man any more than his pack of starving mongrel dogs. But Dixie's point that they knew absolutely nothing about Blue Bullet was well taken. It just seemed as if Johnny Starving Bear was a little crazy and probably wild as a march hare. Furthermore, this business about catching the blue stallion from a tree was ludicrous. Ruff had expected that they would relay the two Thoroughbreds and run Blue Bullet into exhaustion until he was overtaken and captured.

"Wait here," Johnny Starving Bear ordered. "I get horses."

"Just keep those dogs away from these Thoroughbreds,"

Ruff called to the departing Indian.

Johnny Starving Bear went inside his wickiup. A few minutes later, he reemerged with a wife and three children. The children were quite small but the wife was as round as Johnny was skinny.

"Nice family," Dixie said as Johnny Starving Bear vanished around behind the wickiup while his wife and children stared at the white visitors astraddle their tall Thoroughbred horses.

Ten minutes later, the Indian came riding around the wickiup with two of the ugliest ponies that Ruff had ever seen. They were runty and ewe necked, both buckskins. Johnny Starving Bear was riding a Mexican saddle with the huge saddle horn. Draped around it were at least four reatas. Jammed under his stirrup fender was an ancient rifle.

Ruff's lip curled with disapproval. The Indian and his ponies didn't look as if they could stand up to any kind of hard travel.

"Don't say it," Dixie warned.

Ruff bit back a disparaging comment. He was an excellent judge of horseflesh and the pair of buckskins were a study of mistakes. They were narrow chested and knock kneed. Big headed and wall eyed, Ruff could only feel pity for the half-starved beasts. If he could have thought of any reasonable way to dismiss the Indian and ride away with Dixie, he'd have done so without a moment's hesitation.

When Johnny Starving Bear reached them, he pitched a reata to Ruff and said, "Rope horse."

Ruff formed a loop. He had practiced a few times as a kid, but never had the patience for perfecting his throw. Still, he was quite sure that he could rope the Indian's second pony and put on a reasonable show. Whirling the rope around and around, he watched the buckskin's eyes follow the loop but when it was cast, the ugly buckskin ducked its hammer head so quick and low that its chin bounced on the ground.

"Bad," the Indian grunted, reaching out and retrieving his reata. "Very bad."

Ruff seethed. Dixie tried to keep from grinning and Johnny Starving Bear coiled the reata he'd just snatched from Ruff and then waved good-bye to his family.

"Where are we going?" Ruff asked as they started back out of the canyon.

"To catch Blue Bullet," Johnny Starving Bear replied. He measured Ruff's glum expression and began to giggle.

TWELVE

For all his goofiness, it quickly became apparent to Ruff that Johnny Starving Bear did know every inch of this rugged New Mexico mountain country. He led them up wild, seemingly unexplored canyons, over exposed granite ridges and through high mountain passes that taxed even an expert horseman's nerve and ability. Sometimes the Indian would suddenly look up in the sky, see a hawk or eagle, and burst out laughing. It was spooky, but Ruff appreciated the way that Johnny Starving Bear handled his ugly ponies and even dismounted to hike when the going was especially steep or rugged.

Two days of perilous riding brought them into Blue Bullet's territory and from the cover of heavy pine forest, the Indian pointed out to them the mustang stallion's favorite watering place.

"He bring his mares here every three days," Johnny Starving Bear announced. "We catch this time, huh?"

"How?" Ruff asked.

In reply, the Indian selected his strongest reata and then used it to point toward a tree under which the mustang trail passed.

"I don't believe it's possible," Dixie said, voicing Ruff's own reservations. "I mean, what . . ."

"You watch," Johnny Starving Bear said. "Then after I rope stallion, you come quick."

"And do what?" Ruff demanded.

"Rope legs. Throw! Then we blindfold and fix good, huh?"

Ruff expelled a deep breath. "What do you mean, 'fix good'?"

The Indian drew his bowie knife and made a slice at Ruff's groin. The meaning was shockingly clear.

"Now, wait a minute!" Dixie protested. "Jack Grimm wants that stallion not only to race, but to breed! If we geld him, we won't get paid."

The Indian put away his big knife and shrugged. "No fix, maybe blue stud kill rich man."

"Maybe," Ruff said. "But once we deliver him, that's not our problem. Jack Grimm has probably got three or four bronc busters on his payroll."

Johnny Starving Bear must have thought that was very funny because he barked a derisive laugh.

That night, the Indian made them camp almost a half mile from Blue Bullet's watering place. He gathered pine needles and mesquite to crush and smeared them over every inch of his body before he left them to go climb up into the pine tree under which the mustang stallion would pass.

Ruff was not pleased. "In the first place, the stallion will probably spot that Indian and not come within ten miles of this country. In the second place, even if Johnny does get lucky and drop a loop over his head, the reata will either hang the stallion, or break and allow him to escape more wary than ever and more difficult to trap."

"Yes," Dixie agreed, "but you have to admit that Johnny knows a lot more than us about this country and wild horses. I think we should humor him for a week or two and learn all that we can before we consider striking off on our own. I say let's give the Indian a fair chance."

Ruff had to admit that his sister's logic made sense. "All right," he reluctantly agreed. "After all, what choice do we have?"

The next morning just before daybreak, Ruff and Dixie

sneaked up near the watering hole. It was almost an hour before they managed to see the Indian's thin brown form draped along a limb.

"He's like a hungry cougar," Dixie said with admiration. "But I'm afraid that even if Blue Bullet really does drink where Johnny Starving Bear says, he still isn't likely to get a rope on the stallion."

"This whole thing is a joke," Ruff complained. "What we ought to be doing is building some kind of a trap in one of these narrow canyons, then chasing Blue Bullet and his mares into it. That would at least play to our strength—the speed of Cannonade and High Man."

"I wonder how long he can stay perched up in that tree," Dixie mused aloud.

"I guess we're going to find out."

Two days later Blue Bullet led his mares down to drink in the stream. It was midmorning and there wasn't a cloud in the sky. The sun burnished the granite mountaintops and the air was dead still.

"Look!" Ruff whispered, flattening against the ground. "Blue Bullet!"

Dixie had forgotten how truly magnificent the wild stallion was. But now, with its ears pricked forward, head high, step light and cautious, she remembered why Blue Bullet was so prized by everyone who saw him. Flattening on the ground beside her brother, Dixie could feel her heart begin to pound with excitement. She was surprised to see that a fine sorrel mare led the way down to drink while the blue stallion guarded the rear of his band, head constantly moving this way and that as if seeking danger.

One by one the mares went to drink. Blue Bullet, tossing his head and scenting for danger one final time, at last went to join them.

"Why didn't Johnny drop his loop!" Dixie whispered with exasperation.

"He's smarter than I thought," Ruff concluded after a moment. "Johnny is determined to let Blue Bullet drink his fill. A thirsty horse that loads up on water isn't able to run or struggle without great discomfort. Besides, if he lassos Blue Bullet, it might be a day or two before the stallion will allow itself to drink again. With a full belly of water, it won't suffer as much."

And sure enough, when the mares and colts had their fill, they trailed up out of the stream and back under the limb where Johnny Starving Bear lay in wait. The stallion followed. Dixie saw only a flickering shadow of movement in the tree before the Indian's loop dropped to perfectly encircle Blue Bullet's powerful neck.

The mustang stallion exploded into the sky. With a squeal of rage, it bolted for freedom and quickly hit the end of the sixty-foot reata. The entire tree bent toward the plunging, squealing stallion. The great limb to which the reata was fastened and which held Johnny Starving Bear whipped downward and, as the reata slipped outward under the sudden and enormous tension, smaller limbs were sheared away.

"Look at him!" Ruff cried, grabbing his rope. "If the stallion had been tied to the trunk, its neck would have snapped! But that limb is jiggling up and down like a fishing pole playing a giant bass! Look at it move!"

"Look at the stallion," Dixie whispered.

"No," Ruff argued, "look at Johnny Starving Bear!"

The Indian had dropped from his limb with two more reatas and while Blue Bullet was fighting the reata and heavy overhead limb, Johnny was already working up a loop and then sending it snaking toward the stallion's heels. The reata spun around the stallion's shinbones, slipped down, and when Blue Bullet stepped inside, Johnny Starving Bear jerked up the slack.

"He's got him!" Dixie cried.

Ruff was already sprinting forward with his own rope. He glanced sideways to see the last of Blue Bullet's mares and colts disappear through the brush but they didn't matter because, all together, they weren't worth the thousand-dollar reward that rested on Blue Bullet's head.

Ruff had to make two casts before he lassoed Blue Bullet around the neck. By then, the stallion had tripped and fallen. The next few moments were a blur of action as the mustang stallion was overpowered and entangled in reatas until it could do little more than squirm.

"We did it!" Ruff shouted with exuberance.

"*We*?" Johnny Starving Bear asked.

"All right, *you* did it," Ruff conceded. "But no matter, the real work is just starting. In fact, I'm not even sure what to do next."

"Nothing," the Indian said. "We wait three days. Stallion get weak and then we fix."

"Uh-uh," Ruff said. "That's too long. The days are warm and even though Blue Bullet is in the shade of this tree, he'd suffer without food or water."

"That's right," Dixie said in complete agreement.

Johnny Starving Bear gave them a withering look and then he shrugged as if to tell Ruff and Dixie that how they handled Blue Bullet—now that he was captured and helpless—was of little interest or concern to him.

Ruff felt very much the opposite. It pained and saddened him to watch Blue Bullet repeatedly thrash his beautiful head against the earth. The ropes cut into the stallion's flesh and, in some places, drew blood. Over and over the stallion futilely called for his missing mares as it struggled valiantly for freedom. Ruff saw pain and desperation in the outlaw stallion's eyes and it made him feel awful.

"Easy," he crooned. "Just take it easy."

Dixie knelt too close to Blue Bullet and the stallion's long yellow teeth snapped like a bear trap capable of lopping off her hand quicker than the blink of an eye.

"Watch him!" Ruff warned.

Dixie nodded and looked a little shaken. "I don't know if there's any chance we'll ever be able to tame this stallion, Ruff. Catching him was the easy part. How are we going to get him to Jack's ranch?"

Before Ruff could answer, Johnny Starving Bear covered his eyes, making it clear that they must blindfold the stallion. That, coupled with a total absence of food or water, was the Indian's solution to the delivery problem.

"Yes," Ruff said, "we will have to blindfold the stallion. But he's not going to suffer any more than is necessary and if you try to geld him when my back is turned, I'll return the favor. Do you understand?"

Johnny Starving Bear did understand because he cupped his privates and began to giggle. Ruff turned away and so did his sister.

The remainder of that day, they did nothing but watch the stallion squirm and struggle to break the reatas that rendered him so helpless. Ruff tried to talk to Blue Bullet the way his father had taught him. It involved a singsong manner guaranteed to soothe and build trust even among the most rebellious of horses. But the horse talking failed to calm the wild blue horse, once the undisputed pride of Jack Grimm's Thoroughbred stables. That night Blue Bullet finally stopped thrashing its head up and down against the earth, but the fiery gleam of hatred in his eyes burned with undiminished intensity.

"I just don't know," Ruff said, "if this horse will ever be

tamed again. There's a wildness in his eyes that tells me he has too much spirit for freedom."

"That's not our problem," Dixie reminded him. "We've agreed to deliver Blue Bullet and the thousand dollars' reward will give us the chance to start up another Thoroughbred ranch. But not in this part of New Mexico."

"No," Ruff said, turning away from the stallion. "Maybe up in Santa Fe, or even Colorado."

Ruff watched Johnny Starving Bear climb back up the tree and untie his reata. The Indian had deceptive strength and quickness. "I guess I owe you an apology," Ruff called up to the man. "You did what you said you'd do but I had to see it to believe it."

The Indian laughed. It was a high, almost girlish laugh and it upset Blue Bullet so that the stallion resumed fighting his bonds.

"Easy," Ruff said, placing his hand on the wild horse's neck and feeling his rock-hard muscles quiver. "You may have lost your freedom, but at least no more bloody fools will attempt to stun you with a rifle bullet across the neck again. That being the case, maybe you might live long enough to enjoy the easy life of a handsome and proven breeding stallion."

In reply, the stallion snapped at Ruff but the horseman was quick enough to get out of harm's way. And when Ruff glanced at his sister, he could see the worry in her eyes and knew that she was just as concerned as he was about how they were going to deliver Blue Bullet to the Grimm Ranch, some forty or fifty miles away.

All that night Blue Bullet struggled against his bonds and it was heartbreaking to hear the stallion call for his mares. Neither Dixie nor Ruff slept a wink and they were grim and haggard by morning.

The night before, Ruff had fashioned a blindfold and while the Indian held down Blue Bullet's head, Ruff applied it. Once blinded, the stallion temporarily lost his will to fight. He quieted while Ruff tied his right foreleg up to his barrel.

"Let's get our horses and we'll lead him seesaw between us," Ruff explained to his sister.

"Do you really think it's necessary to tie his leg up like that?" Dixie asked, clearly troubled.

"Yes, at least for the time being," Ruff said. "Otherwise, he'd throw himself at one of our horses and we'd have a hell of a wreck. Most likely, it would come in some bad place on the trail and we might even get knocked off a mountainside."

"But if it's forty or fifty miles . . ."

"I don't like it, either, Dixie," Ruff said, fully aware of what a terrible physical hardship it would impose on Blue Bullet, "but my aim is to put the welfare of our own horses first. And once on the trail, I think we ought to just keep Blue Bullet moving and not stop until we reach Grimm's ranch."

"Good plan," Johnny Starving Bear said, nodding his head in agreement.

Ruff mounted Cannonade and Dixie mounted High Man. Together, they dallied the reatas around their saddle horns and when they had tension, Ruff called, "All right, Johnny, let's get him up on three legs!"

The Indian quickly loosened the reatas that bound Blue Bullet's hind fetlocks together, leaving just two reatas around the wild stallion's neck. For a moment, Blue Bullet lay still, eyes unseeing before surging to its feet. Almost falling, it corrected its three-legged balance and displayed enormous courage by leaping forward, albeit hobbled and blindfolded.

"Hang on!" Ruff shouted, leaning back in his saddle and hoping that Cannonade knew enough to brace himself for the shock that was about to hit the end of his reata.

Cannonade was not ready and neither was High Man. When the wild blue stallion hit the end of the reatas, both Thoroughbreds were practically jerked off their feet before they regained their balance and dug in their heels. Blue Bullet crashed to the earth but climbed back to his feet, squealing and snapping. He lunged toward Dixie but Ruff pulled him back. Turning and squealing with rage, Blue Bullet charged Ruff but Dixie and High Man drew the wild horse up short. For ten nerve-wracking minutes, Blue Bullet fought the two ropes and the men and horses that held him suspended. After three more punishing falls, the captured stallion seemed to realize the futility of his efforts. His flanks were dripping with sweat and his sides were heaving. The ropes had partially choked off his airway and he was having difficulty breathing.

"Ease up a little and let's give him some air," Ruff ordered.

Dixie urged High Man a step forward and the ropes slackened. Both she and her brother held their breath and prayed that Blue Bullet would relax and then allow himself to be led down the trail.

"He good boy now!" Johnny Starving Bear shouted happily. "He tame now."

"Not hardly," Ruff said. "He's probably just getting a second wind."

"But how in the world are we going to do this where the trail narrows!" Dixie wailed. "And how can he possibly negotiate bad stretches of trail on just three legs!"

"We'll find a way," Ruff promised, without having a real answer. "Maybe I'll have to ride up front and you behind. As for that raised foreleg, after a few miles, I'm hoping he'll be worn down enough so that we can drop it. We'll just take things a step at time. But even if it takes a week, we're going to deliver a tired but healthy Blue Bullet to the Grimm Ranch. And the three of us are going to have a big, big payday."

Dixie seemed to take heart at these words and within a few minutes, they had the wheezing blue stallion moving forward, toward Jack Grimm's beautiful ranch in the valley of Rum River.

THIRTEEN

When Jack Grimm saw Johnny Starving Bear leading the procession of three stallions and two riders, he shouted, "They captured Blue Bullet!"

The ranch hands came rushing forward to gather around their boss. When they observed Johnny Starving Bear galloping ahead on one of his ugly buckskin ponies, everyone grinned.

"I'll bet anything that crazy Indian is the one that found and finally outwitted Blue Bullet," Dick Hastings said.

"That might be," Grimm answered, "but it's Dixie and her brother that are in control and delivering Blue Bullet to my bronc pen. Dick, open the gate and let's get that stallion inside. Make sure that he has hay, grain, and water! I don't want to pay these folks a thousand dollars for a dying horse."

"Yes, sir!"

Ruff and Dixie were glassy eyed with exhaustion and the still-blindfolded Blue Bullet looked beaten until he caught the scent of a paddock full of frisky and curious Thoroughbred mares. Perking up, the outlaw stallion bugled his arrival and began to prance. It was all that Dixie and Ruff could do to negotiate Blue Bullet into the high, round-sided bronc pen. They had long since removed his hobble and now they did the same with his blindfold, escaping before Blue Bullet could exact his revenge on either the weary Cannonade or High Man.

"So," Grimm proclaimed, "you caught him!"

"Actually," Ruff said, "Johnny Starving Bear caught him. We just brought him home."

"You did what no one else could do," Grimm said, "and I'm a man of my word. You'll be paid that thousand dollars and maybe you'd also like to earn a handsome sum of money by breaking him."

"No, thanks. Just pay us the thousand dollars."

"All right," Grimm said, peering through the corral gate once more. "You and Dixie come up to the house."

"Me too," Johnny Starving Bear said with a happy grin.

Grimm cast a questioning look to Ruff, who explained, "We agreed to pay him a third."

"A third? To a crazy Indian!"

"That was the deal. And like you, we honor our agreements."

"He'll just squander the money. Probably get drunk or get beaten and rolled in town."

"That's his choice." Dixie fumed. "But he still gets a third."

"Hell, I don't care!" Grimm shouted, turning to march back toward his house. "The reward's cut into your shares. But I'll have no dirty, crazy Indians in my house."

Johnny Starving Bear's dark eyes shuttered, then he glanced back toward the pen, which now held Blue Bullet. Ruff thought that he detected anger, possibly even regret on the Indian's hatchet-shaped face.

As they were walking away, Ruff called back, "Johnny, we'll bring you your share of the money, don't worry."

Once in Grimm's office, the rancher wasted no time in opening his safe and counting out the promised reward money. "As you can see, I'm a man of my word. Now, what about our horse race?"

"As soon as High Fire is fit, we'll talk about it," Ruff announced shortly. "But it has to be a fair race."

"Sure, sure," Grimm snapped with impatience. "I've got a new man coming in from Santa Fe to ride Cannonade and he'd better win. He's the best jockey in the business and when he wins next Sunday, I'll buy Cannonade back from you for one hundred dollars."

Ruff cocked his eyebrows up in question. "You said he was worth a thousand."

"That was before he was beaten by your eighteen year-old stallion!" Grimm said bitterly.

"And what if Cannonade loses?"

"Then I don't buy him and neither will anyone else." Grimm's voice dropped a little and it grew hard with a warning. "And furthermore, Rufus Ballou, your future suddenly—and permanently—goes very sour. Do you get my drift?"

Before Ruff could explode in anger, Dixie ushered him outside. "Just settle down."

"I'll be damned if I'll race a Ballou horse that isn't allowed to win!"

"Can we talk this over tomorrow?" Dixie pleaded. "Ruff, we've just gone through hell delivering Blue Bullet. All I want to do now is to go to town, check to see how High Fire is recovering, get a hotel room, and get some sleep."

Before Ruff could respond, Johnny Starving Bear came between them, palm upraised and extended.

"Here you go," Ruff said, counting out exactly $334 for the Indian. "Johnny, I'd strongly advise you to go back home and hide that money. Everyone knows that you've got it and it's a strong temptation for evil hearts."

Johnny Starving Bear rubbed the thick stack of greenbacks against his bare, bony chest. He giggled and did a little shuffle in the dirt as he raised his hands and flapped his arms like a bird.

"Crazy as a loon," Grimm grumbled, coming out of the house in time to witness the Indian's antics.

"Except when it comes to catching wild horses," Ruff said, remembering how magnificently the Indian had laid his trap and then caught Blue Bullet.

Ruff waited until the Indian stopped dancing and waving his arms. He laid his own hand on Johnny Starving Bear's shoulder and said, "Go on home."

For the first time since they had met, the Indian's face grew somber and the mirth left his eyes. Then he said in a low, confidential voice, "Go to hell, white man."

Ruff blinked with the sudden realization that Johnny Starving Bear wasn't a bit crazy. He might be a little odd, but it seemed entirely likely that the Indian had created a persona of lunacy so that white men would not take him seriously and even avoid rather than torment him.

Waving a fistful of cash, Johnny Starving Bear trotted over to his ponies, leaped onto one's back, grabbed the lead rope to the second, and galloped off toward Rum River.

"You watch," Jack Grimm said with contempt. "That Indian will be busted by tomorrow morning. You did him no favor."

Ruff was afraid that there was truth in Grimm's dismal assessment. "Come on, Dixie," he said, "let's get out of here. We can ride High Man double back to town."

But Grimm wasn't through speaking. "I've paid up your livery bill at Dobler's and I'll keep paying him until Sunday. Your young stallion is fit, I've had daily reports on him."

Ruff had to bite his tongue to keep from giving the rancher a piece of his mind. The only thing that kept him quiet was the realization that Jack Grimm still held all the cards and could no doubt create a reason to have him arrested and thrown back in jail.

That night, after getting good hotel rooms and hot baths, the Ballous celebrated their hard-won fortune. Nothing outrageous, but they ordered the best steak-and-potato dinner offered in Rum River. Ruff even ordered wine to wash his dinner down.

"We did it," he said, raising his glass in a tribute to their accomplishment in capturing Blue Bullet. "Dixie, now we've got a chance to build our new horse ranch like Father would have wanted."

"Yes," Dixie said, "but I just keep thinking about Blue Bullet. How sad he looked and how much hell we put him through."

"We saved his hide," Ruff contended. "Sooner or later, someone would have shot him either hoping for a neck stun, or out of pure frustration and meanness."

"You're probably right."

"I know I am. And I'm glad we're the ones that caught him and got the reward. Furthermore, I'd like to return to that wild horse country and see how many of his mares we can capture. Most of them are Thoroughbreds that belong to Jack Grimm and I'll bet he'd pay plenty to have the best of them returned to his paddocks."

"I suppose. But we'd probably need Johnny's help again, wouldn't we?"

"I'd ask him to join us for another equal share. But if he refused, I'd still want to give it a try by ourselves."

Dixie chewed thoughtfully. "So what are we going to do about the race?"

"May the best horse win," Ruff said. "How could it be otherwise?"

"If High Fire beats Cannonade, we're back in the dog house—or worse. My point is, we'd have to just keep running because Jack would find a way to get even."

"Fine," Ruff said, "then we forget Blue Bullet's scattered band of mares and just keep running. But it can't be a crime to fairly win a horse race."

"In this part of the country," Dixie said, "I think it's probably a prison offense to do anything that riles Jack Grimm."

Ruff was about to say that he didn't give a damn about Grimm when suddenly, he heard two quick gunshots out in the street. Jumping up from the table, he rushed to the door and looked outside. It was dusk but the light was not so poor that he could not see three men firing bullets at Johnny Starving Bear's feet while the Indian hopped and danced.

Ruff drew his own six-gun.

"Be careful!" Dixie begged.

But Ruff wasn't feeling in a very "careful" mood. Especially when he realized that one of Johnny Starving Bear's tormentors was none other than the ex-deputy, Bert Flagg.

Ruff was totally focused on the three men as he stepped outside and brought the barrel of his Colt crashing against one of the men's skulls, dropping him like a shot ox. Before the other two could react, Ruff's left hand connected solidly against flesh, and then only Bert Flagg was standing, smoking pistol in his fist.

"Go ahead," Ruff challenged the ex-deputy, "make your play so that I'll have plenty of witnesses to testify that I shot you in self-defense."

There was an unmistakable edge of hopefulness in Ruff's voice that seemed to chill the reckless anger in Bert Flagg. His gun clattered to the boardwalk.

"You shoot me, it'll be murder," Flagg warned, taking a back step.

"You should have left town for good when you were warned by Dick Hastings that he'd shoot you on sight,"

Ruff growled. "Maybe you could have run far and fast enough so that I'd never have found you, but I'd always be looking."

"Ballou, we got no quarrel. And as for the injun, well, we was only having a little sport."

"I see," Ruff said, holstering his gun.

Flagg's eyes dropped to his own pistol. Ruff smiled. "If you want to go for it, by all means, do so."

The ex-deputy licked his lips and his mind waged a titanic struggle, but in the end, reason prevailed. "No, thanks. It wouldn't be a fair fight."

Ruff shrugged. "And neither was the one in the jail cell when you beat the hell out of me while I was handcuffed."

Before the man could form a reply, Ruff doubled up his fist and smashed Flagg in the nose. The nose popped and gushed blood. Flagg's howl abruptly ended when Ruff planted a wicked left hook into the man's solar plexus. Flagg's cheeks blew out and his eyes bugged as he jackknifed forward, gasping for air. Ruff sledged him behind the ear and the ex-deputy hit the boardwalk so hard he bounced.

"Be gone by tomorrow morning or I'll kill you," Ruff vowed, looking over at Johnny Starving Bear.

The Indian wasn't giggling now. In fact, tears washed by moonlight shone across his cheeks.

"Go on home," Ruff said gently. "And stay out of Rum River if you value your health."

"I still have money," the Indian said, swaying only a little.

"Then consider yourself a fortunate man."

The Indian hiccuped, reeled about, and swayed off, trailing vapors of whiskey as he headed for his ponies.

Ruff surveyed the damage he'd wrought, then took his sister's arm and steered her off down the boardwalk. "We'll get some sleep and rest up for a few days while we measure exactly what kind of shape High Fire is in for Sunday's race."

"You've had plenty of time riding Cannonade," Dixie said. "Can High Fire outrun him?"

"Yep. If he's feeling up to snuff, I sure wouldn't bet against him."

Dixie tried to smile but failed.

"What's the matter?" Ruff asked.

Shrugging her shoulders, Dixie replied. "Even if we win the race, we lose because Jack will have you arrested. And if we lose, we lose and humiliate High Fire. If you deliberately hold a racehorse back, sometimes they never trust you again or try to so hard to win. So it just seems to me that there's only bad news no matter what happens on Sunday."

"We just run an honest race and let the best horse win," Ruff said. "That's what our father would have done in this position and damn the consequences."

"Yeah," Dixie said, "but that doesn't make me feel any better or worry any less."

FOURTEEN

High Fire still wasn't feeling right on race day. Ruff fussed and fumed and vacillated between calling off the race and going ahead with it until midmorning, when he made his decision.

"I'm calling the race off," he told Dixie as they left Dobler's Livery for their hotel rooms. "High Fire isn't fit to run yet. Furthermore, he's out of condition and I'm not going to take any unnecessary chances with his health."

"All right," Dixie said. "But I think that you know what is going to happen when Jack finds out. We've got a town full of people expecting a horse race and they're going to be up in arms."

"Let them be," Ruff snapped. "When Grimm arrives, I'm going to explain why we won't race High Fire and then I'll ask to be paid a fair price for Cannonade."

"You mean more than the hundred dollars?"

"That's right. We won that horse and we'll take him with us if Grimm can't do better than a hundred dollars."

Dixie shook her head doubtfully. "I think you're pushing the man in a corner and he'll fight."

"Fair is fair," Ruff said stubbornly as they marched up the street toward their hotel with a gathering crowd of bettors filling the streets. They'd already decided to vacate their rooms, store their few belongs at Dobler's, and then leave Rum River immediately after their announcement to Jack Grimm. In that way, they hoped to avoid any chances of Ruff being arrested again on some trumped-up charge.

"Hey!" a shrill voice cried. "Wait up a minute, I need to talk to you!"

Ruff and Dixie turned to see a tall, buxom, and auburn-haired woman hurrying after them. "Who is that?" Ruff asked.

"That's Tina. She's Jack's girlfriend."

"What do you think she wants?"

"I haven't a clue," Dixie said, "but don't worry. Tina isn't the kind to mince words. Whatever is on her mind, she will tell us straight out."

"Big woman," Ruff said, coming to a halt and then tipping his hat.

Tina, wearing high heels and a plumed hat, was almost tall enough to look Ruff eye to eye. "Do you know what Jack told me he intends to do now!"

"No, ma'am."

"He intends to substitute Blue Bullet for Cannonade in today's race."

"What!" Ruff took a back step. "He can't be serious!"

"Well, he is," Tina said. "They fitted that horse with blinders and his cowboys rode that wild sonofabitch down so that Jack thinks he can be ridden in today's race. He's got a Santa Fe jockey that is a real hotshot. Between that wild horse and this Santa Fe jockey, Jack figures he's guaranteed a race victory."

"The race is off," Dixie said. "High Fire is not in condition to run."

"Good!" Tina declared. Then, turning around and cupping her hands to her mouth, she bellowed loud enough to be heard up and down the street, "The race is off! Everyone, the race is off!"

Sheer bedlam followed this announcement until Ruff was forced to jump up into the back of a wagon and call for silence. When that didn't work, he drew his six-gun and drilled holes in the sky. "Everyone, shut up!"

The crowd fell into a grudging silence. Ruff cleared his throat and said, "Our young stallion is still not in running condition! We won't risk his health. I'm sorry, but the race is definitely off."

"Then race your old one against Cannonade again and, this time, you give Grimm's horse a head start!"

The crowd gave a loud belly laugh and Ruff sighed with relief. He was about to explain that Grimm had decided to race the famed Blue Bullet when he spotted Jack Grimm and his cowboys entering town leading the blindfolded outlaw stallion. On his back was what Ruff guessed was the Santa Fe jockey, and the man looked half-terrified as the crowd stampeded toward him to get a better look at the famous wild stallion.

"Uh-oh," Ruff said, hopping down from the bed of the wagon. "Here comes big trouble."

"Why don't you just up and leave on the run while there's so much commotion?" Tina suggested.

It wasn't a bad idea. Ruff had seen Blue Bullet run and he was more than a match for the gallant old High Man. In fact, given his extraordinary condition, he might even whip a healthy High Fire, though it would be a extremely close.

But right now, Blue Bullet was approaching a state of near panic as the excited and overexuberant crowd pressed in around him, hands reaching to touch the famed wild horse that had confounded every attempt to catch him until he'd become a New Mexico legend. The Santa Fe jockey screamed for the people to get back, and when one actually tried to pluck some hairs off Blue Bullet's tail as a souvenir, the stallion went crazy. Rearing up, he lunged forward, knocking people down. Faster than the strike of a snake, a rear hoof sent the man who had stupidly plucked his tail flying through a storefront window.

Blue Bullet trampled another man and then charged onto the boardwalk. The jockey on his back attempted to control Blue Bullet but the insane stallion took the bit in his mouth and crashed through the paper-thin front wall of the nearest saloon. Ruff winced to imagine the mayhem that Blue Bullet was unleashing inside that dim and cluttered saloon. He heard shouts of terror and saw men flying out of the place like fleas bailing off a dying dog. Some were hurt, all were in a high state of panic. Only Dick Hastings and three other veteran Grimm Ranch cowboys had the presence of mind to shake out their loops and gallop their cow horses forward.

When Blue Bullet came charging back outside, two things were missing: his blindfold and the Santa Fe jockey. Dick Hastings was an expert roper and his whirling loop caught the blue stallion's forelegs and pitched the stallion into the street. The other three cowboys quickly had their lassos around the fighting outlaw's muscular neck.

Blue Bullet somehow managed to struggle back on his feet just as Ruff swung onto his back. He took the reins and yelled, "Everyone, get back!"

Jack Grimm, however, was not about to allow himself to be upstaged. He jumped forward and tried to grab Blue Bullet's bridle as he yelled, "Get off of him! He's my . . ."

Whatever Grimm was about to say was silenced as the stallion's long yellow teeth clamped onto the rancher's chest. Grimm screamed and Ruff was helpless as the Blue Bullet shook the rancher as a cat might a rat. He hurled Grimm to the earth and would have finished him off if Ruff hadn't been able to saw the outlaw's head around and slap his Stetson across his eyes. Then Dick Hastings and the other cowboys were using their skilled cow ponies and ropes to drag Blue Bullet off his feet again. Ruff kicked out of his stirrups to hit the ground rolling. He was the first one to reach Jack Grimm's side.

The rancher was barely conscious. His fancy coat and shirt were ripped from his bloody chest. Not only had Blue Bullet bit him, but he'd stepped on the downed rancher, and Ruff feared that Grimm had sustained fatal internal injuries.

"Get back!" Ruff shouted at the crowd as Blue Bullet thrashed and fought his ropes nearby. "Get off the street!"

The next few minutes were a cacophony of noise and confusion. Ruff ordered for someone to bring a stretcher. He was aware that Tina was practically suffocating the rancher and weeping hysterically. She even drew a derringer and emptied two shots at the helpless Blue Bullet but only managed to wing a bystander.

Somehow, they finally got Jack Grimm into the hotel and upstairs to Tina's room. Ruff tore off the man's bloody coat and shirt. He took Grimm's pulse and noted from his dilated pupils that the rancher was in shock.

"We need to keep him warm and quiet," Ruff said, wishing that there was a real doctor in Rum River instead of the drunken Zacky.

"Is he going to live?" Tina asked, pale with worry.

"I don't know. His color is poor but his pulse and breathing are good and strong."

Grimm's eyes fluttered open. "Shoot him. Shoot him!"

"Are you talking about Blue Bullet?" Dixie asked with surprise.

"Yes, kill him!"

Dixie and Ruff exchanged alarmed glances. "Don't worry about that stallion," Ruff said. "He'll be taken care of. It's you that we're worried about."

But Grimm's head rolled back and forth on his pillow. He tried to raise on his elbows and he looked straight at Ruff. "I want that killer stallion gut-shot!"

"Take it easy," Ruff warned. "How bad are you hurt?"

Grimm fell back, groaning and gasping for breath. "I . . . I don't know. I think my ribs are broken."

"Ribs mend. Let's just hope that that's all that was damaged."

"That chest wound needs doctoring," Tina said, staring at the big tear in Grimm's flesh. "My God, you'd think that stallion was a grizzly, the way he opened up poor Jack!"

"Clean it out good and use some sulfa or iodine," Dixie suggested. "Then keep it bandaged. It will leave a bad scar, but it'll heal."

"Morphine," Grimm sobbed. "I need morphine!"

"I'll find some," Tina promised. "One of the girls has the habit. Don't you worry, honey, everything will be all right."

Ruff nodded to Dixie and they left the room. Dixie grabbed Ruff's arm and spun him around in the hallway. "What are we going to do now!"

"We've got a tough decision to make," Ruff informed her. "We either steal Blue Bullet and risk going to prison, or we live with the knowledge that we caught a wild horse that should have remained free."

"We can't let them gut-shoot Blue Bullet! That horse was just trying to break away. And with all those fools pulling at his tail and—"

"I know," Ruff interrupted "But we both heard the hatred in Jack's voice. As soon as he comes out of shock and later the morphine, he'll order Dick Hastings to shoot that stallion."

"Then we must save him!"

Ruff sighed. "Stealing back that horse would put us in prison for sure. Why, it's likely even a hanging offense!"

"So what are we going to do?" Dixie demanded. "Just turn our backs on all of this?"

"I don't know," Ruff confessed, taking his sister's arm. "But at least we didn't have to rig a dishonest race for Cannonade to win."

"Yeah," Dixie said, "with all the excitement, I'd completely forgotten about the race."

Ruff said nothing more until they were back down in the street. By then, the cowboys had managed to get a blindfold back on Blue Bullet and were leading the fighting stallion off to the Grimm Ranch.

A huge crowd was gathered before the saloon that Blue Bullet had demolished and the Santa Fe jockey was unconscious and bleeding from the ears, telling Ruff that he had a severe concussion, and maybe a lot worse. Other people were still on the ground, some covered with blood, others just battered and in various stages of shock. Fortunately, none were women or children. The whole scene of devastation reminded Ruff of a little Tennessee village he'd once seen that had been leveled by a powerful tornado.

"One horse," Ruff muttered, shaking his head with near disbelief.

"He's not a horse!" a merchant who had overheard Ruff's remark choked with bitterness. "He's a devil that God has sent to punish Rum River for its sinful ways!"

"No," Dixie said, "he's just a horse that's tasted freedom and is willing to die in order to have it back. He's no different from some people in feeling that way."

The man, heavyset and cradling his left arm as if it had been broken in the havoc that had so shaken this town, cursed, "Damn that evil blue devil!"

Ruff took his sister's arm and led her off toward Dobler's Livery. "We're leaving while we can," he said. "There's going to be nothing but hell to pay in Rum River when Jack Grimm comes around."

"But what about Blue Bullet! We can't let him be shot!"

Ruff came to a standstill and looked deep into his sister's eyes. "So what are you suggesting?"

"I'm not *suggesting* anything! I'm telling you that I won't leave this valley if Blue Bullet is going to be gut-shot!"

Ruff knew his sister. She was a mule for stubbornness and she never bluffed. If Dixie said that she was not going to leave Blue Bullet to be shot, that was exactly what she meant.

"All right," he said. "We'll free the horse."

"When?"

"How about tonight?"

Dixie relaxed. "We can't afford to wait any longer than that. By tomorrow, Jack might be awake and able to give the order to Dick Hastings."

"What if he changes his mind?" Ruff asked, his mind working furiously. "What if, once he has settled down and no longer is in shock, the man decides to change his mind and keep that stallion? Maybe just for breeding?"

"I . . . I hadn't thought of that."

"Well, we need to," Ruff declared firmly. "If that were the case, we'd have needlessly branded ourselves as horse thieves."

"Maybe we should just take Blue Bullet, hide him someplace, and then wait to see what happens," Dixie suggested.

"As if we don't already have enough troubles with four Thoroughbreds."

Dixie slipped her arm though Ruff's arm. "We just have to do what is right," she said. "And what our conscience dictates. It's the way our father taught us to handle tough decisions. It's the way that we know is best."

Ruff couldn't disagree. But he sure wished that, instead of waiting until dark to steal the outlaw stallion, they were riding north to Santa Fe and putting Rum River and all this trouble behind.

Yes sir, it seemed that just as they were about to escape one mess, they bought into another.

FIFTEEN

Ruff and Dixie peered out from behind the cottonwood trees that traced the meandering path of Rum River. Sunset was melting like butter across the crown of the Mogollon Mountains. Two miles distant, Jack Grimm's mansion gleamed as white as pup's teeth and the air was warm and hazy soft. Crickets chirruped along the lazy river and an owl hooted, anticipating his hunting hour.

"It's not going to be easy," Ruff told his sister. "There's no cover other than the paddock fences and outbuildings. And I doubt that Blue Bullet is going to be cooperative."

"I wish we could just sneak in, open his gate, and then run for it," Dixie said, "but you know that he'd return to his mares and he'd be shot on Jack's orders."

"Yes, but even if we can get that horse out of here without rousing the entire crew tonight, we still haven't the faintest idea of where we should take him. To keep Blue Bullet from returning to his home range, we might have to lead him blindfolded all the way up to Colorado."

"Ruff, let's play it one step at a time. If we can free Blue Bullet, let's take him to Johnny Starving Bear's hidden canyon. I'm sure he'll have some idea of what to do with such a famous stallion."

"He'll probably just want to geld him. That's what he wanted to do before and it might be the only answer to saving the horse from self-destruction."

"What a waste!" Dixie exclaimed. "A horse like that ought to be passing on his bloodline."

133

Ruff supposed that was true, although he wondered if Blue Bullet's outlaw disposition might also be passed along to the detriment of future generations. To Ruff's way of thinking, it didn't matter if you had the fastest horse in the world if the animal was too mean or treacherous to handle. He'd seen vicious Thoroughbreds before and they were a menace to the other horses and riders and soon were banned from racing. Ruff's late father, Justin Ballou, had always believed that disposition, like speed, color, and conformation was an inherited characteristic and one that should be taken into account when selecting sires and dames for breeding.

"Ruff?"

"Yeah?"

"Do you ever think about going back to Tennessee when the war is over?"

"Sometimes." Ruff watched the last rays of light fade from the land. "But to be honest, I don't believe we'll ever again see the South we knew and loved. I think if we went back there would be nothing but heartache and destruction."

"What about Houston?"

The reminder of his next oldest brother was a painful one to Ruff. Against all of Ruff's pleading and arguments, Houston had ridden north seeking a young woman he'd fallen in love with and had apparently been captured and imprisoned. No doubt, Houston would be held as a prisoner until the end of the war. There was not a day that had passed since word had arrived from Houston telling them about his sad circumstances that Ruff had not considered going north to try and free Houston from his harsh federal prison. But each time, he'd come to his senses realizing that his first responsibility was to Dixie and the last of the Ballou Thoroughbreds.

Ruff sighed. "I think that someday we'll see Houston riding up looking as tall and handsome as ever. And who knows, maybe he really will have found love and want to settle out West and help us rebuild what we lost in Tennessee."

"You always were an incurable romantic," Dixie said.

"I'm not very pretty with a missing earlobe."

"Aw, that don't account for anything," Dixie told him. "You're still a handsome enough fella. It's just that you're sort of rough around the edges. Your name fits, if you know what I mean."

"Yeah, I guess," Ruff said, unable to keep from comparing himself to his handsome older brother or someone like Jack Grimm who, before he'd been hurt by Blue Bullet, had cut quite a fancy figure with his nice clothes and charming manners.

Frowning, he added, "Trouble is, Dixie, I always seem to be in such a bad fix that I can't imagine dragging a woman through all of my trials."

"Well, what do you think I am!"

Ruff, realizing his mistake, grinned. "I didn't mean you any offense. You're family, Dixie. Besides, the reason we're here now is that you couldn't bear to let them shoot Blue Bullet."

"And you could?"

"No," he admitted, "of course not."

Ruff turned back to the horses and checked High Fire's cinch. Dixie would be riding High Man and they'd leave their two brood mares here in the trees and collect them on their way north—baring the very real possibility that they were discovered trying to steel Blue Bullet and apprehended by Dick Hastings's ranch crew.

"There's one thing," Ruff said. "If we do rouse the troops, we split up and I'll try and draw away the chase on High Fire. You return here, collect our mares, and strike out to the east. We'll meet up by that saddleback."

Ruff pointed out a distant saddleback in the silhouetted ridge of mountains parading to the east. "Is that understood?"

"Yes," Dixie said without argument. "But I think we can do this without being caught."

"I hope so," Ruff said. "Let's saddle up and get moving. In about six hours the sun will come up again and, even if this goes without a hitch, that's when someone is sure to notice that Blue Bullet is missing. I expect it will cause quite a stir."

"I'll take the lead," Dixie said, mounting High Man. "I know the ranch's layout and how to reach Blue Bullet without putting ourselves in any more danger than necessary."

Ruff fell in behind his sister. The stars were a blanket of diamonds and the moon was a drop of sweet honey. It worried Ruff that his sister was riding in the front and he had to keep reminding himself that this was not the terrible Civil War where a startled sentry would shoot an intruder on sight. No, this was just a ranch where a bunch of hard-riding cowboys earned their pay and slept like the dead until dawn.

As they rode quietly past the Jack Grimm's buffalo herd, Ruff marveled at the huge creatures. When Dixie led them through the maze of whitewashed paddock fences, Ruff could see the fine Thoroughbred mares with their colts and fillies sleeping nearby. It reminded him of their own Ballou paddocks once so lovingly attended back at Wildwood Farm in Tennessee. All gone, just like his father and brothers.

God damn all wars.

At last, they came to Blue Bullet's bronc pen—the high-walled and solid-sided one that was supported by tall, thick treelike posts.

"He's in there," Dixie said, riding up to the gate. "Now what?"

"I don't know," Ruff confessed. "If I ride into that pen on High Fire, there will be a hell of a fight. If I go in on foot, I'm a dead man. You tell me."

"You mean you really don't have any idea of how to get that horse out of there!" Dixie asked with obvious disbelief.

"That's right. Short of opening the gate and taking a throw at him with my rope. And even if I got lucky and caught him by the neck, then what? He'd twist around and attack and we'd have a hell of a wreck. You know how he'd squeal and raise hell. It'd wake up the whole ranch and we'd be caught red handed."

"Well, then exactly what are we going to do?"

"I think we just ought to open the gate and let that stallion run away. Tomorrow or the next day, we can try to catch him again," Ruff said, thinking aloud. "We could be at Johnny Starving Bear's canyon by daybreak and on Blue Bullet's trail a few hours later."

Dixie's sigh was audible. "All right," she said. "Then we'll just have to do it that way, but I have to tell you that I'm less than impressed."

"Don't matter none to me whether you're impressed or not," Ruff said, feeling slightly offended. "The main thing we got to think about is not getting caught and branded as a couple of horse thieves."

Ruff rode up to the gate. He heard Blue Bullet whinny and then stomp his feet in a challenge to High Fire. Ruff's stallion nickered and then squealed and Ruff figured that there was no time to be wasted because there was already a fight brewing between the two Thoroughbreds and it would be loud enough to awaken every man on the ranch.

Ruff opened the gate and got out of the way fast as Blue Bullet charged out of the bronc pen, kicking and snorting. The stallion ran about fifty yards, then angled toward a paddock holding the three Thoroughbred mares. Before Ruff or Dixie could react, Blue Bullet whirled and kicked the fence to pieces, then rounded up the mares and drove them into the night.

"Let's get out of here!" Ruff called, seeing lanterns go on in the bunkhouse.

Dixie needed no urging. She sent High Man racing off through the paddocks, riding low so that her body would not be silhouetted against the starlight. Ruff followed suit and he prayed that no one would see them racing away and that Dick Hastings and his crew would simply assume that Blue Bullet had escaped by his own devices.

When they reached the cottonwood trees, the Thoroughbreds were blowing and still plenty excited. Without conversation, they untied their brood mares and rode hard, making an enormous circle to the west and then lining out for Johnny Starving Bear's canyon.

At daybreak, they watched sunrise flow across the caprock dome of a ten-thousand-foot mountain. Breaking a silence beginning with the release of Blue Bullet, Dixie said, "Can you believe that stallion emptied that paddock of its mares before he escaped for freedom?"

"I sure can," Ruff said. "Maybe he is a devil."

"When Jack finds out that he's lost three more of his best brood mares, he'll go crazy," Dixie predicted. "I think it points out that, more than ever, we have to get that stallion out of this country. I'll bet that Jack puts another reward on his head, only this time it will be for the first man who drags his blue hide back to the ranch."

Ruff was pretty sure that Dixie was absolutely correct. "Well," he said, "let's just hope that Johnny Starving Bear has a few more horse-catching tricks. I doubt that Blue Bullet is going to fall for being lassoed from a tree again."

Dixie tugged her Stetson down tight and blew a tendril of black hair that had fallen across her eyes. "Come on," she said, "let's see if we can get Johnny to help us save that blue stallion even though there's no reward to be earned this time."

Ruff had his doubts about the Indian. Johnny Starving Bear might prefer to live isolated with his family in a wickiup but he still liked money and he'd be less than eager to risk his neck saving an outlaw stallion in the name of human kindness and mercy.

SIXTEEN

Even before Ruff and Dixie arrived at Johnny Starving Bear's hidden canyon, they could smell smoke and the stench of death. Ruff glanced at his sister and read the apprehension that he also felt building inside.

"Maybe he's just roasting a bear or something," Ruff said hopefully.

"Maybe."

When they passed through the narrow defile of two sentinel rocks, Ruff drew his six-gun and Dixie dug her own pistol out of her saddlebags. Dismounting and tying their horses, they went ahead on foot, expecting the worst.

"Oh, my God!" Dixie exclaimed. "What have they done to these Indian people!"

Ruff lowered his Colt and shook his head. Nearest to him were Johnny Starving Bear's two ugly buckskin ponies, both shot. The bodies of Johnny's dogs were scattered everywhere, most obviously blown apart by shotgun blasts. Behind this carnage was a smoldering ash heap where the Indian's wickiup had once stood. And beyond that sat Johnny's wife and three small children, looking frozen with shock.

When they saw Ruff and Dixie, they recoiled with fear. "We're friends!" Ruff called as Dixie handed him her reins and hurried ahead on foot.

Ruff watched as his sister attempted to comfort and reassure the badly frightened Indians. It was evident that they did not understand English, and Dixie's smattering of Spanish didn't seem to be having an effect, either. Dixie was forced to use sign language while Ruff watered their horses.

After an hour or so, the Indian woman relaxed and became very animated. She kept pointing southward and her face was a mirror reflection of her anxiety and hopelessness. Ruff guessed that Johnny Starving Bear was probably dead, maybe buried or lying out in the brush someplace, murdered and robbed for his share of Blue Bullet's reward money. The miracle was that the Indian's wife and children, though admittedly poor witnesses, had been spared.

At last, Dixie returned. "It's bad," she said. "As near as I can tell, three riders struck at dawn. They shot their dogs and horses, then captured Johnny. They took what money he had left from the reward and then ransacked the wickiup, looking for the rest."

Dixie shook her head and continued. "When they didn't find it, they threatened to kill the entire family. I guess Johnny pleaded for mercy and told them that he could catch Blue Bullet's entire band of Thoroughbred mares. He convinced his captors that the mares were worth a lot of money and they would be easy to trap."

"Could you learn who the three men were?"

Dixie nodded. "I think so. The woman drew two stars in the dust."

"Stars?"

"That's right. And then she tapped her breast. I think you can guess their names."

"Ex-Sheriff George Watson and ex-Deputy Bert Flagg."

"That's right."

"It makes sense, Dixie. Both men were kicked out of office and sent packing. I guess they saw a chance for some easy money before they left this part of the New Mexico Territory. I can't quite picture that fat ex-sheriff trying to catch wild Thoroughbred mares, but Bert Flagg was game for anything. And the third man might be a real mustanger."

"So what are we waiting for?" Dixie asked. "They have a good six-hour head start. Trouble is, our horses are already tired."

"We'll leave the mares here," Ruff decided out loud. "Tell Mrs. Starving Bear that in return for their feed and watering, we will do everything we can to bring back her husband alive and in good health."

Dixie hurried to rejoin the Indian family. After a few minutes, Mrs. Starving Bear and her children came and led the brood mares back deeper into the canyon, where Johnny had built a pole corral for his buckskin ponies.

"She will take good care of them," Dixie said.

Ruff had no doubt that this was true. Before he remounted High Fire to ride back out of the canyon, he waved to the poor Indian family and he was heartened to see that the little children waved back. It was a good omen, Ruff thought. Now, if they could just overtake the mustang-hunting party and save Johnny's hide before Blue Bullet showed up to reclaim his mares.

"What are you thinking?" Dixie asked after they'd ridden several hours in grim silence.

"I was thinking about Johnny."

"And . . ."

"I was thinking that Watson and Flagg believe that Indian is crazy, which he is not. And that, if I was those men, I'd be damned afraid to turn my back on Johnny, given what they did to his family, dogs, and ponies."

"I was thinking the very same thing," Dixie confessed. "Johnny Starving Bear has a way of making you believe he is almost harmless and helpless. But nothing could be farther from the truth. If I were any one of the three men that took him away, I would be on my guard every waking moment."

"If Johnny tries to kill those men, and I'm sure he will, he'll only have one chance and he'd better get all three at the same time."

"That seems like a tall order."

"Maybe so," Ruff admitted, "but this is Johnny's country. He knows every inch of it and he'll wait and strike when the land and his surroundings give him the greatest possible advantage."

"What about the band of mares?"

"Perhaps Johnny has no intention of leading his three captors anywhere near Blue Bullet's mares. Fortunately, his captors are expecting pursuit and their tracks will be easy to follow."

"Look!" Dixie exclaimed, reining High Man up shortly, then dismounting. "They must be driving Johnny ahead of them on foot!"

Ruff had already seen the faintly outlined moccasin tracks that marked the hard ground.

Dixie remounted her old Thoroughbred stallion. "With Johnny on foot, we ought to have no trouble overtaking them."

Ruff glanced up at the sun and judged they had another four hours of daylight. After that, they could probably keep tracking their quarry by moon and starlight. With any luck, they'd come upon them before dawn and finish this thing once and for all.

Forty miles to the southwest and higher into the Mogollon Mountains, Johnny Starving Bear stood at the edge of a cliff overlooking a deep, red gash of canyon. The sun was dropping quickly and dark shadows raced across the canyon floor, blanketing the silver thread of water that could be still seen in the fading light.

"Down there," Johnny told the three men who had whipped, ridiculed, and driven him like a burro.

He raised his hands that were bound together at their wrists and pointed downward toward the canyon floor. "That is where we will find the Blue Bullet's mares."

"Well gawdamn," Bert Flagg swore. "How the hell do we even get down to the bottom of that deep sonofabitch?"

"I know the trail," Johnny assured them. "It is close. We follow tomorrow."

"We still got almost an hour of daylight," Watson argued. "Why don't we ride on down tonight and catch them hot-blooded mares first thing in the morning?"

"Bad idea," said the tall, angular man with the eyes of a hawk and the stringy muscles of a mountain lion. "Even if the damned trail started right here, we'd still get caught on it in the dark. I don't guess any of us want to risk a tumble over the side, do we?"

"Hell no," Watson grumbled. "But, Yancy, you know as well as Bert and me that the sooner we trap those purebred mares and get the hell out of this part of the territory, the better it will be for all of us."

In reply, Yancy dismounted and loosened his saddle cinch. He pulled his saddle free, exposing the wet square of his horse's back. Throwing his saddle down, he left no doubt that this was to be their camp for the night.

"This will have to do for now," was Yancy's comment. "Least it will be for me. Ain't going to risk my horse on some damned mountain goat trail in the dark."

His horse was a big buckskin whose outstanding looks promised quickness, speed, and stamina, like the man himself. Both the man and his horse stood above and apart, things cut from a different mold than either of the two ex-lawmen. In contrast to their apprehension and uncertainty, Yancy gave the impression of being a man at ease with the wilderness. His eyes were blue-gray and shuttered low under heavy brow. His jaw was square and wide, like his shoulders. He was lean hipped and a trifle bowlegged.

"Sheriff," Flagg said, using the title out of habit, "I say we make use of what light we have and get on down to the bottom of that canyon."

"Well, I dunno," the fat man replied. "Yancy might have a good point about not wanting to get caught on the side of a cliff."

"Sure I do," Yancy drawled. "Deputy, what you don't seem to realize is that some things can't be rushed."

"I didn't ask you for no lecture!" Flagg stormed.

"Maybe you need one," Yancy said, eyes tightening at the corners but voice still congenial. "For you see, kid, we jest haven't got a man or a horse to lose if we're going to catch that stallion's band of expensive Thoroughbred mares."

Bert Flagg, chafed from the long ride, was in an irritable and contrary frame of mind. "Dammit, don't call me 'kid'! I told you that twice already! Me and George are runnin' this show, not you. And I say—"

"Shut up, kid," Yancy drawled. "You're just blowin' hot wind and makin' no sense."

The rebuff was so casual that young Bert Flagg's jaw dropped and hung suspended a moment before he remembered to snap it shut. "I don't like you!" Flagg hissed. "I don't know why the hell you was even asked to come along."

"Because George knows that I'm the only one of us white folks who understands a damn thing about wild horses," Yancy patiently explained. "And because, if the Indian starts to playing games, I'm the one that'll punch his ticket first."

"You been acting like you're the boss or something," Flagg snarled in anger. "Fact is, you're just along for the damned ride."

"Hey," Watson pleaded, "let's not start wrangling among ourselves."

"Suits me," Yancy demanded. "I just have damned little tolerance for a fool."

"You calling me a fool!" Flagg bellowed in a challenge.

"If the name fits, then wear it."

Flagg glanced at the sheriff. When he realized that Watson was not going to interfere, he decided to go for his gun. The move was anticipated by Yancy, who stepped forward and smashed the ex-deputy in the face. Flagg's gun never cleared its holster.

The deputy of Rum River staggered, regained his footing, then lowered his head and charged. Yancy coolly stepped out of the man's path and drove his fist into Flagg's kidney as he swept past. The deputy grunted and doubled up with pain but stayed on his feet.

"You had enough?" Yancy asked.

When Flagg went for his gun again, Yancy's pistol whipped up in his fist to belch death. The deputy was lifted onto his toes, still gripping his holstered pistol. His face turned slack with amazement as he stared down at the rosy red stain starting to blossom across his chest.

"Jeezus!" Flagg wailed, looking in vain at his sheriff for help. "George, the murderin' sonofabitch shot me!"

In reply, Yancy shot him again, this time in the belly. Flagg screamed and Yancy kicked forward and booted him in the gut. Flagg's shriek carried him over the edge of the cliff and abruptly ended when his body caromed off a boulder, crashed through deadfall, and sheared branches off a pine tree far below.

"Damnation!" ex-Sheriff Watson exclaimed. "You didn't need to kill him!"

"He was worthless," Yancy pronounced, holstering his smoking pistol and then rubbing his skinned knuckles. "Worse than worthless. At least you have brains enough to know you're a fish out of water in this rough country and that you have to listen to your betters—the kid didn't even have that much sense. He'd have fouled up our chances of catching them high-priced Thoroughbred mares."

Watson gulped. "Remember, Yancy, I saved your neck from being stretched once. You wouldn't—"

"Kill you, too?" Yancy's laugh had a cold, hollow sound as if it were belching up from the bottom of a deep, dark well. "Naw! I'll need some help beside the Indian's and . . . Johnny is gone!"

"Sonofabitch, he *is* gone!"

Johnny Starving Bear had seized the opportunity to escape during the fight. Not only was he gone, but so was the single-shot carbine that had been hooked by a leather thong from Bert Flagg's saddle.

"He could have shot us!" the sheriff cried.

"One of us, not both. And whoever was left would have killed him before he could get onto a horse and run. That's why he ran off."

"Well, what . . ."

But Yancy was already swinging onto his buckskin and spurring along the edge of the cliff. He did not gallop fifty yards before he saw the fleeing Indian and yelled, "Up there! See him! He's heading for that canyon trail. Come on, we got to get him first!"

Johnny Starving Bear heard Yancy's shout and when he glanced back over his shoulder, he saw the tall horseman riding bareback and spurring forward. The buckskin was flying, its stride long and powerful. Johnny knew that he would be overtaken in less than a minute and that there was no chance for him to reach the steep, narrow trail that switched back and forth down into the canyon below.

Because of his wife and children, Johnny rejected the impulse to throw himself off the cliff and thwart the white men. Instead, he sprinted toward a boulder just ahead. When he reached it, he slammed the single-shot rifle down and tried to take aim on the tall horseman. Accuracy was impossible, given that his wrists were tied together. Rather than try to kill the rider, Johnny aimed at his buckskin horse, a much safer target. He hated to do it but he squeezed the trigger and saw the buckskin collapse as a ball entered its broad chest. The horse somersaulted across the rocky ground. Yancy hit the earth rolling and would have stopped and gained his footing if he hadn't suffered the grave misfortune of being having his thigh impaled by the thick, sharp branches of a dead and fallen tree.

Yancy bellowed. Johnny dropped the carbine, grabbed a rock, and would have rushed to bludgeon the tall horseman, except that Yancy was conscious and still able to draw his six-gun. The tall man opened fire, and his shots whistled by Johnny's head and made him change both his mind and direction. With every ounce of his failing strength, Johnny raced away, following the edge of the cliff until he reached the canyon trail. It was steep and so treacherous enough that only a fool would attempt to descend it on horseback instead of leading his animal.

Johnny threw himself down the trail hearing shouts and gunfire ringing in his ears. He did not know if the one called Yancy was fatally injured or not. All he knew for certain was that Bert Flagg had possessed a knife and a six-gun when he'd toppled over the edge of the canyon and crashed to the canyon floor.

And to Johnny's way of thinking, if he could get his hand on a knife to cut the rawhide that bound his wrists, and then find the ex-deputy's six-gun, he'd have nearly an even chance of getting revenge. The gun and the knife were all that Johnny Starving Bear concentrated upon as darkness dropped like the giant lid of a cast-iron kettle upon the canyon land.

"I'll get you! You killed my damned horse and you'll pay, you crazy sonofabitch!" Yancy cried over and over, voice ricocheting back and forth across the canyon.

Johnny Starving Bear halted and craned his head up toward the rim of the canyon, listening to the tall man scream. And when at last Yancy's cry for vengeance became a mere ragged whisper, Johnny threw back his head and giggled. His wild, womanish giggling floated over the great chasm beyond and caused the night birds and animals to huddle, frozen in their hiding places.

SEVENTEEN

When High Fire's ears pricked forward and the stallion halted dead in its tracks, Ruff's hand flashed to the butt of his six-gun and his heart skipped a beat. After a few tense moments, Ruff thought he heard a faint, off-key noise carried on the wind.

High Fire stamped his feet nervously and Ruff looked to his sister. "Did you hear it?"

"Hear what?"

"I dunno," Ruff admitted. "High Fire heard it and then I was sure that I also heard something. It was like . . . like a calling."

"Was it like a shout or a scream?"

"I wish I could say, Dixie. I just caught a snatch of it on the wind."

Dixie's eyes tightened. "I hope it wasn't Johnny Starving Bear being tortured. In a few minutes, it'll be dark."

"There will be enough moonlight to follow these tracks," Ruff assured his sister. "Sheriff Watson, Bert Flagg, and whoever the third man is aren't worried about being followed. But we'd better go slow and easy from now on. Judging from the tracks and that last pile of horse manure, I'd guess we aren't more than two hours behind. We've been closing the gap all afternoon."

"I just hope that they aren't doing terrible things to poor Johnny," Dixie continued to fret. "Anyone who would shoot a man's dogs and horses wouldn't hesitate to resort to torture."

"I'm expecting a gun battle," Ruff admitted. "And when it starts, I'd like your promise that you'll stay out of harm's way."

"Not a chance!" Dixie lowered her voice. "If you think that I'm going to hide in the bushes while you take on three cutthroats, you have another thing coming, Rufus Ballou! We're in this thing together all the way."

Ruff knew that it was useless to argue with Dixie. Besides, she was a pretty fair shot with pistol or rifle and she would even the odds. With luck, perhaps they could get the jump on their quarry and not have to fire a shot in order to free the captive Indian.

For the next two hours they picked their way carefully along the trail, pausing often to listen for a voice or the nicker of a horse or perhaps even snoring. Judging from the stars up above, it was nearly eleven o'clock when High Fire's head jerked up in the air and his ears riveted forward again. A low rumbling nicker started to build in the stallion's chest and before it could develop into a full-blown whinny, Ruff dismounted and clamped his hand over High Fire's nostrils.

Dixie didn't have to be told to do the same with old High Man to keep him quiet.

"They must be just up ahead," Ruff whispered. "I'm going to go on ahead and scout around."

"Oh, no, you don't!" Dixie hissed. "Not without me!"

"But . . ."

"I mean it. We can crush the leaves of these smelly bushes and wrap scented bandannas around the muzzles of our horses. That ought to keep them from bugling."

"If it doesn't," Ruff said, "we'll walk into an ambush."

"That's the chance we'll both just have to take," Dixie said with such an air of absolute finality that Ruff abandoned the idea of argument. Dixie further displayed her resolve by taking her Navy Colt out of her saddlebags.

"Are you sure it's loaded?" Ruff asked skeptically.

"Of course!"

She jammed the Colt in behind her waistband and tore a handful of leaves off a nearby bush. Wrapping them in her bandanna, Dixie scrubbed them against her leg and then dumped them on the ground.

Raising the bandanna to her nose, Dixie made a face in the moonlight. "Our stallions can't possibly smell any other horses now," she judged, wrapping the pungent bandanna around High Man's muzzle. "Come on, Ruff, what are you just standing there gawking for? We haven't got all night!"

Ruff curbed his annoyance. It galled him that his kid sister should be ordering him around in a time of great danger. "Just remember who's in charge," he said lamely. "I'm going to give these fellas a chance to surrender. Best way to handle this is if there's not a shot fired."

"I know that, Ruff! But if we stand here talking all night, they're liable to get up at sunrise, have coffee and a nice leisurely breakfast, then ride on before we even get moving!"

Ruff ground his teeth in silent anger. He removed his bandanna, reaching for some leaves and twigs to crush. It really was irritating to have to endure the company of a brave but bossy fifteen-year-old girl. When High Fire was taken care of to Ruff's satisfaction, he drew his six-gun and started forward at a running crouch. He stayed to the trail of the Indian and his three ruthless abductors until he saw a large, dark silhouette of unfamiliar proportions lying on the trail up ahead. Skidding to a halt, Ruff crept slowly forward until he realized that he was staring at a dead buckskin mare.

"Damn," Ruff muttered under his breath. He motioned Dixie forward and they skirted the fallen animal, moving from rock to tree while keeping low and trying to avoid making even the faint sound of a turning rock under their booted feet.

"There they are," Ruff whispered, as they crouched behind a boulder and peered through the darkness.

"I only see two sleeping figures."

"The other two must be just below that rimrock."

"So what do we do now?"

Ruff took a deep breath. "We can either try and take them now, or wait until first light."

"I say we do it now and get it over with," Dixie argued. "There's enough moonlight to see what we are doing. If we get the drop on them while they're asleep, they'll be groggy, confused, and more likely to surrender."

"Makes sense," Ruff admitted. "But we still have to locate the other two before we make our move."

"Why don't you circle around and see if you can find and disarm them? If anything goes astray, I can open fire from here and we'll have them in a cross fire."

Ruff had to admit that it was a reasonably good plan. Or at least it was logical. "All right," he said, "just stay low and don't do anything unless I yell for help. And don't shoot me by mistake!"

"You're the tall, slim fella," Dixie said. "I'd recognize your silhouette in a minute. Don't worry, I won't accidentally shoot you, Ruff."

"Good." Ruff reached out and gave his sister an awkward squeeze. "I know that you'll do just fine," he said, "but if something should go wrong, then promise me you'll return to the Thoroughbreds and run for your life."

"And leave you!"

"Only if I'm dead," he told her, then added quickly, "but that won't happen."

"Then why bring it up!" Dixie snapped. "Now go on!"

Chastised, Ruff began to sneak around the camp. The way he figured it, he had to find the other two men before making any kind of a move. It would also help if, before he tried to get the drop on these boys, he knew which of the sleeping figures was Johnny Starving Bear.

But after fifteen minutes of tense searching along what Ruff now realized was the edge of a deep canyon, he still had not located the other two men. Ruff didn't understand. What could have become of the other two? Had they gone on ahead for some reason? It didn't make sense but Ruff had the feeling that time was running out. Dixie had even less patience than he did and by now she'd be squirming with anxiety, finger itchy against the trigger of her pistol.

Ruff decided that the best thing to do was to circle the camp and rejoin Dixie. Then, they could sort out the confusion and decide what to do next. But just as he was about to start moving again, one of the sleeping figures sat up, then unfolded heavily to his feet. One glance told Ruff that this was the mysterious and as yet unidentified third man, and that he had suffered a grievous injury, for he limped, obviously in great pain. But even doubled over, he was obviously much taller than either the ex-sheriff or deputy. There was plenty of moonlight to see that he was a big, wide-shouldered man with a wedge-shaped face and the bowed legs of a man very, very familiar with a saddle horse.

Ruff held his breath as the man picked up a holster and gun to hobble over to the edge the canyon. For a long time, he stood gazing down into the dark chasm, then he turned and hobbled back to check the two horses. Apparently satisfied, he started to crawl back into his bedroll.

But something caught his attention and he froze, then flattened against the earth. Ruff took a deep breath and held it. He was hiding not fifty feet from the big man and

there could only be one explanation for his sudden alarm—
Dixie. Sure enough, confirming Ruff's worst suspicion, the
big man began to slither off in Dixie's direction.

Ruff was momentarily paralyzed by fear for his kid sister,
a fear as chilling as a pail of ice water. But then, as the tall
man cocked back the hammer of his pistol, Ruff jumped
forward and shouted, "Freeze!"

The tall man twisted around and fired in the same motion.
Ruff felt the bullet whip-crack past his missing earlobe as
he squeezed off a succession of shots so rapidly that their
retorts blended like rolling thunder. The big man's body
jerked as hot lead slammed into his chest.

When he collapsed, Ruff started forward. Dixie appeared
like a spirit from a hole in the earth. "Look out behind
you!"

Ruff dropped and rolled as a bullet kicked dirt skyward.
He fired and knew he'd missed as George Watson's gun
bucked again in his pudgy fist.

Dixie's own pistol was barking and on the second shot,
the former sheriff of Rum River was lifted to his toes. Like
a comic ballerina, he pivoted as both Ruff and Dixie's
guns exploded again and sent the man tumbling backward
to suddenly disappear into the canyon.

Ruff jumped up and ran to his sister. "Are you all right?"

"Sure," Dixie said breathlessly. "But where are the other two?"

"I don't know," Ruff answered, realizing he'd forgotten
all about them. He reloaded, then stared at his sister. "You
just saved my life."

"And you saved mine. I never even saw that tall man
until he was practically on top of me!"

Ruff flopped over onto his back and gazed up at the
stars for a moment with a tide of relief flooding through
his veins. "We both got lucky. Real lucky."

"But what about Johnny!"

"I don't know. I just don't know. All I *do* know is that I didn't see him or Bert Flagg. Maybe they already climbed down into that huge canyon. Or maybe the trail down is so steep and narrow they both fell to their deaths on the rocks below."

"But . . ."

"Dixie," Ruff breathed, "stop asking so many questions and offer a prayer of thanks that we are still alive. It could just as easily have gone the other way for one, or both of us."

"I guess you're right. So what are we going to do now?"

"Nothing until daybreak."

"And then?"

"Then we'll find Johnny Starving Bear and Bert Flagg. Maybe dead, maybe alive."

"I think they're dead," Dixie said quietly. "I think that Watson and that big man murdered them. Don't ask me why, it's just that there isn't any other logical explanation."

"Perhaps not," Ruff said, closing his eyes and wondering if he dared risk a nap until sunrise.

"Are you going to go to sleep and leave me sitting here all awake and alone!" Dixie protested in outrage.

"You won't be alone."

"Well, it's not fair!"

Ruff struggled to sit up. He glared back at Dixie. "Can *you* sleep?"

"Are you kidding! After what just happened? Hell no!"

"Well, I can," Ruff informed her. He laid back down and drew his hat over his eyes.

"How can you be so . . . so inhuman!" Dixie asked with amazement. "We just kill two fellow human beings, see a dead horse, and . . . and almost get killed ourselves and . . . and you go to sleep?"

"I'm dog tired, Dixie. Be quiet. Keep your pretty brown eyes open and your pretty big mouth shut so you can listen."

Dixie punched him. Punched him in the ribs hard enough to elicit a painful grunt. But Ruff didn't move and as soon as Dixie quit muttering and swearing, Ruff figured that he would have no trouble dropping off to sleep.

EIGHTEEN

The sun was well above the eastern peaks when Ruff opened his eyes. For a moment, he lay half-asleep, savoring the pine-scented mountains and crisp, thin air. But then, remembering the circumstances of the previous night, he started into wakefulness.

"Dixie? Dixie!"

"Stop yelling," she called from the edge of the cliff overlooking the great canyon below.

Ruff struggled to his feet. He saw the tall horseman's body lying exactly where he'd collapsed the night before and again realized how fortunate he and Dixie were to be alive. Knuckling his eyes, he staggered over to his sister, who was sitting with her legs drawn up and chin resting on her knees. Dixie's eyes were fixed on the canyon floor and Ruff just naturally followed them. He immediately saw big George Watson's corpse splattered across a flat boulder. But then he saw another body.

"Well, I'll be," Ruff whispered, "that's Bert Flagg!"

"Yes."

Ruff's eyes scanned the canyon floor far below. "Any sign of Johnny Starving Bear?"

"No." Dixie raised her hand to point. "But unless my sleep-starved eyes are betraying me, isn't that Blue Bullet and his mares grazing near the end of this huge box canyon?"

Ruff had forgotten to put on his hat and the rising sun was bright enough to make him raise his hand to shield its glare. "Why, it sure is!"

"If Johnny is alive, that's where we'll find him," Dixie said. "Now, all we have to do is to figure out if we want to descend a goat trail I found leading down into that canyon, or ride an extra ten or fifteen miles out of our way to get down there without risking our lives."

"I don't know," Ruff said, "why don't you show me this so-called goat trail and I'll give it some thought."

Dixie showed him the trail and it took Ruff about ten seconds to form an opinion. "I wouldn't go down that ant track even if I had wings and could fly!"

"Good," Dixie said with relief. "I guess a wild horse or a burro might navigate it, but I sure wouldn't expect it of High Fire or High Man. Besides, we have three extra horses to worry about now."

"That's right," Ruff said. "And three bodies to either bury or pack into Rum River."

Ruff noticed a couple of turkey vultures circling high overhead. "I guess they already got wind of last night's festivities."

"I'm wondering if they also see poor Johnny Starving Bear," Dixie fretted. "His body could be hidden anywhere in those trees or rocks below. If they'd pitch Bert over, they'd do the same to that Indian."

"Not likely," Ruff argued. "The reason they took him in the first place was to help them catch those wild Thoroughbred mares that once belonged to the Grimm Ranch."

"Maybe they just took him to show them *where* to find Blue Bullet's harem," Dixie suggested. "Has that occurred to you?"

"No," Ruff admitted, "it has not. But I doubt they'd kill Johnny, given how good he was at catching wild horses."

Since there was only one way to find out, they loaded Yancy's body onto a horse and Ruff led off to the west. He hoped that they would only have to flank the rim for about ten or fifteen miles before they could find the entrance to the great horse canyon below.

It was well past noon and the New Mexico sky was warm and cloudless when Ruff finally reined High Fire through some heavy timber and found the wild horse trail leading into the great hidden box canyon. The trail was a deep furrow and there were fresh tracks, no doubt those of Blue Bullet and his latest collection of Grimm Ranch Thoroughbred mares. Ruff twisted around in his saddle and would have smiled at Dixie except for Yancy's body draped across the back of the sheriff's saddle horse.

"We've found it now," Ruff called, letting his stallion pick its way along the steep and narrowing trail that fed along a stream. Higher and higher they climbed into what looked as if it were itself a dead end until they arrived at a narrow defile in the rocks filled with a cold, clear stream.

"This is just like the one that we passed through going into Johnny's canyon!" Dixie called.

"Narrower and wetter," Ruff said, actually forced to pull his stirrups in tight against High Man's ribs in order to keep them from hanging up on the high rock walls that guarded the canyon. "In the spring, I'll bet so much water flows through here that you can't get through. Probably have to hike that 'goat trail' you pointed out to me."

"Probably," Dixie said, following up the rear and wincing as Yancy's long, stiff legs were almost torn off by the narrow walls whose rough surface was matted with horse hair.

"So what are we going to do if Johnny isn't in here?"

"I dunno," Ruff conceded. "But I tell you one thing, there's a couple thousand dollars' worth of blooded horses trapped in this canyon and I'm going to make damn sure they don't escape while we're figuring what to do with them."

"Makes sense," Dixie said.

When they passed through the narrowest part, Ruff used the sheriff's rope to lasso a big fallen branch, which he made High Fire drag over to block the canyon's entrance.

"That' isn't going to stop a horse like Blue Bullet," Dixie said. "He'll fly right over the top of it."

"Probably right," Ruff said, untying his rope and going for another branch.

A half hour later, they had a high, almost solid wall of branches across the canyon's entrance. "It's going to take some work just to get ourselves back out of this place," Ruff said.

"We'll get out," Dixie assured him. "It'll all get removed faster than it got stacked."

Ruff figured this was true enough. He recoiled the sheriff's rope and looped it over his saddle horn before remounting his horse. Taking the lead again, he rode into the canyon knowing that it would not be long before Blue Bullet and his mares were aware of their presence.

"Let's stay in the trees all the way to the place where Bert and the former sheriff landed," Ruff said. "Then we'll take a look and see if we can spot the Indian."

Dixie nodded, feeling a little pale with the thought of so much death. And a short time later, when she saw the condition of the rock-battered corpses, she nearly got ill.

"I'll go on up a little ways," she said, "just in case Johnny was pitched off the goat trail."

"Good idea," Ruff told her.

And as soon as Dixie was out of sight, he dragged all three bodies over to the canyon wall at a place where there was a long shale rock slide. He laid Yancy, Bert, and George head to toe like three pieces of cordwood, and then attacked the rock slide, bringing down tons of shale to cover the bodies.

Sliding back down to solid ground, Ruff felt compelled to remove his Stetson, close his eyes, and say, "They weren't much, Lord. All three were meaner than weasels. But they must have had a mother that loved 'em when they were young. And maybe they had good fathers that tried but failed to teach them about decency and honor. At any rate, I commend them to your care and trust you'll not send them to an everlasting hell. But thy will be done, Lord. Amen."

Ruff slapped his hat back down on his head and heaved a sigh of relief to have the burying done. He'd made up his mind that he was never going to return to Rum River. But Johnny Starving Bear had been a good man and it would only be right to return his body to his wife and kids for a proper Indian burial before leaving for Colorado.

And then, just as Ruff was slapping the dust from his pants, he heard a high, familiar giggle. Whipping his head around, he saw Dixie leading her horse and beside her was Johnny Starving Bear, grinning as if he didn't have a lick of good sense.

"Johnny!"

"White man!"

Ruff chuckled. "What are you doing down in this canyon all by yourself? Figuring on catching that blue stallion and collecting another reward?"

The Indian nodded but said, "Maybe we catch all horses together, huh?"

"Suits me," Ruff said. "But I'm not of a mind to return that blue stallion to Rum River so that a half-crazed rancher can have him gut-shot."

When Johnny shrugged his thin shoulders, indicating he did not understand, Dixie explained all about Jack Grimm's disastrous decision to race the blue stallion against High

Fire. She ended up by saying, "When Blue Bullet took a bite out of Jack's chest and shook him like a terrier would a rat, I thought that he would rouse the dead because of his hollering."

The Indian laughed so hard he had to hug his sides and Ruff laughed hard for the first time in weeks. Dixie, however, did not even look amused. "I've been horse-bit on the chest and it's not funny."

The two men laughed even harder until Dixie's icy glare silenced them. She said, "What did you do with the bodies?"

Ruff's smile evaporated. "I gave them a proper burial under that pile of shale. I even said a few words to the Lord. I think they'd have been pleased."

"I doubt it," Dixie said. "But maybe it's for the best. We couldn't have dragged a wild horse within fifty yards of three corpses. There was no way that we could have captured those horses and returned those bodies to Rum River for burial."

"That's the way I saw it," Ruff said agreeably. He looked to Johnny. "How do you figure we can get a couple of lassos on that big blue horse again? I doubt he'll walk under another tree for you."

The Indian shrugged his shoulders. "We leave him. No reward. Take mares instead. They easier to catch."

Dixie's expression reflected her concern. Ruff guessed his sister was troubled by the thought of taking the mares and leaving the stallion trapped in this canyon. "Maybe if we get the mares, the stallion will trail along behind, Dixie."

"Do you think so?"

"I don't know," Ruff said honestly. "But it's possible. And Johnny is right, the mares are the ones that will bring us money. And while most of them were Jack Grimm's

Thoroughbreds, there are a fair number of just plain old mustangs in the band."

Ruff turned to the Indian. "How do we do this?"

Johnny Starving Bear did not answer Ruff's question but instead climbed onto the sheriff's saddle horse and rode back to the entrance to the canyon.

"What is he doing?" Dixie asked.

"I don't know. But he'll tell us when he's ready."

Fifteen minutes later, the Indian galloped back and dismounted. He knelt in the dirt and, using a stick, quickly drew a sketch of the canyon and its entrance. "Here," he said, pointing his finger at the entrance, "is where we build a catch pen. Drive mares in, then rope."

"There must be thirty mares," Dixie said. "How are we going to control them all?"

"Keep blooded mares, let others go free."

Ruff understood at once that Johnny Starving Bear was making excellent sense. The Thoroughbred mares were the real money horses. And since they were formerly tamed, they'd not be difficult to gentle again and lead north. In addition to Johnny's reatas that they'd found up on the rim, the three dead men had all brought lariats. Ruff also had one and so did Dixie. That meant that, together, they had probably two hundred feet of hemp rope and braided leather reata. They'd be able to fashion halters for the mares and leads, and they'd do just fine.

"Time is wasting," Ruff said. "I just wish we had a couple of axes and some tools to build a catch pen with, Johnny. It's going to be a booger without them."

But the Indian shook his head. "Rope more limbs and drag with horses. You watch, catch pen easy."

Ruff nodded and grinned. Johnny Starving Bear wasn't the same man that he'd been earlier. Now, he was serious and without any pretense of being crazy, though Johnny retained a very odd sense of humor, causing him to giggle at the strangest times.

As they set to work, it was understood that they needed to build this catch pen in a hurry and trap Blue Bullet's mares. After all, given Jack Grimm's obsession for vengeance, it seemed certain that another reward was out on the blue stallion's head and greedy horse killers were already on the move.

NINETEEN

Ruff had never built a catch pen before and wasn't sure exactly how large it would have to be or even if its opening wings were supposed to be camouflaged. All he knew for certain was that the catch pen would have to be stout enough to withstand the impact of some pretty big and fast Thoroughbred mares driven down from the high end of the canyon.

But Johnny Starving Bear knew exactly what was required. He showed Ruff and Dixie how to use heavy rocks to anchor the limbs and small trees that he managed to rope and drag to the canyon's mouth.

"Pile them as high as your head," he warned, "or these tall horses will jump over the top. One will knock some branches down and the others will knock the rest. It must be tall enough so that there is no jumping. Thick enough so that the mares can see no opening to break through."

Ruff saw the Indian's logic. His years of working with horses told him that often, the mere illusion of a solid wall was enough to stop a charging horse or intimidate one that wished to escape. A horse could not distinguish thickness. That was why even a blanket draped over a rope would usually fool an animal into thinking he was contained by a solid and impenetrable wall.

"I don't think I've ever worked so hard in my entire life," Dixie grumbled on the second afternoon when they had one thirty-foot-long wing of the trap completed.

"It sure would be easier with a couple of axes," Ruff repeated for perhaps the twentieth time. "This evening I'm

166

going to ride up the canyon and get a closer look at Blue Bullet and his mares. You want to come along?"

"Sure," Dixie grunted, helping her brother drag a heavy limb into place. "I haven't seen Johnny all morning, have you?"

"He left in the night to visit his wife and children. I noticed that he took both Watson and Flagg's saddle horses."

"Can't blame him for that," Dixie said. "Do you think he intends to collect his family and bring them back here?"

"The thought has occurred to me."

"Might be the best thing to do," Dixie conceded. "If I were him, I'd be worried that someone else would pay an unexpected and unpleasant visit on his wickiup in the hope of stealing the rest of Johnny's money. He'd better bring our two brood mares if he and his family abandon that little wickiup and canyon."

"He will."

Dixie wiped sweat from her brow. "I'll say this about Johnny Starving Bear, he has good timing and plenty of sense to escape this drudgery. Far easier to just lay out what needs to be done and then ride off and let us slaves do all the labor."

Ruff had to chuckle at his sister's sarcasm. Around horses, Dixie was happy to work from dawn to dusk, but piling wood and rocks up to construct these wings was another matter. Yesterday, Johnny had used a heavy branch to mark exactly how the wings of the trap should curve slightly outward from the canyon's entrance. And he'd just as clearly shown that he was not interested in building the wings himself. Instead, he'd spent most of his time on horseback scouting for wood to be used for construction. By lassoing logs and limbs, the Indian could deliver more building material in two hours than Ruff and Dixie could stack in an entire day of hard, difficult labor.

"We're not slaves," Ruff said. "If we wanted, we could ride off to Old Santa Fe and or even Denver City, where there's supposed to be a big gold rush."

"Well, that's what we ought to do, then," Dixie grumped. She studied her hands, which were covered with pine pitch and blisters. "This is miserable work. I got ticks and ant bites all over me and I'm ready to hit the trail north."

"Not me," Ruff said, rubbing his own blistered hands together reflectively. "You see, Dixie, while we have a few hundred dollars left over from getting paid for capturing Blue Bullet, that isn't nearly enough money to purchase the kind of a spread we've been dreaming about ever since we were wrongly chased out of Tennessee. But if we can catch this band of Thoroughbred mares, and even after giving a third of them to Johnny, we'll have something pretty special. We can take them north and either sell or keep a few of the best, adding new blood into the Ballou line. Those mares will be the key to our success, Dixie. We need 'em."

"Jack Grimm might have something to say about that," Dixie warned. "He thinks they still belong to him."

"They don't. They belong to whoever is good enough to catch them," Ruff argued. "Hell, if that weren't the case, why'd he pay a thousand dollars for the capture of Blue Bullet?"

Dixie could follow Ruff's logic and she sure wasn't about to go to all this work just so they could hand the mares over to Jack Grimm.

"I wonder how Jack is feeling," Dixie asked. "He looked to be in real bad shape the last time we saw him in Rum River."

"He's a survivor. I'd bet my bedroll that Jack Grimm is doing just fine and has already announced his reward for the killing or capture of Blue Bullet."

"I'm glad that we're in this hidden canyon," Dixie said. "There's not much chance of us being found, is there?"

Ruff scowled. "I don't know. That afternoon thunder-shower that we had yesterday probably wiped out the tracks we left coming over from Johnny Starving Bear's place. At least, I hope that it did."

"And if someone spots Johnny?"

Dixie had hit upon the very concern that had been nagging at Ruff all morning. And while he tried to comfort himself in the knowledge that Johnny was wily and would be smart enough not to highlight himself on the ridges, it was also true that one mounted rider leading a pair of saddle horses would attract both the eye and the attention of anyone scouting for Blue Bullet in the hope of winning Grimm's bloody reward.

"Johnny is too careful a man to let himself be spotted," Ruff said with more confidence than he felt. "And my guess is that he'll be back with his family sometime tomorrow or tomorrow night."

"I'll feel easier when they're all back safe and sound."

"Me too. And you know who worries me the most?"

"Who?"

"Dick Hastings."

Dixie scoffed. "Dick is a fine man! Even if he did get lucky enough to stumble onto this canyon, he loves horses too much to shoot Blue Bullet."

"I hope you're right," Ruff said. "And while I'm sure that he does appreciate good horseflesh, seeing his boss get nearly stomped to death by Blue Bullet might have changed his opinion about that stallion. And then, too, Hastings isn't a young man and he needs to keep his foreman's job."

"I think you're wrong about the man," Dixie said. "And anyway, we'll have those mares and be out of here long before anyone has a chance of finding this hidden canyon."

"Hopefully," Ruff said, going back to the hard work of building the horse trap's long second wing.

That evening Ruff and Dixie saddled their Thoroughbred stallions and rode up the canyon to where they had a good view of the wild stallion and his band of mares.

"You can see the new mares that he captured last week after busting down the fence and getting into Grimm's paddock," Ruff said. "Quite frankly, you have to admire the bandit."

"Do you think Blue Bullet will ever be tamed again?"

"I doubt it. That blue stallion loves the taste of freedom too much to ever give it up again. I wouldn't want to keep a horse like that, always thinking he was trying to figure out a way to toss me over a cliff or into a cactus patch in order to escape. My hunch is that Blue Bullet would rather die than give up his freedom again."

Ruff pointed. "Do you see that grulla and the family of three roans? I'll bet they're true wild mustangs. If they have foals out of Blue Bullet, they're going to throw top-quality colts. Horses that will possess a Thoroughbred's size, strength and speed but also be blessed with a mustang's legendary stamina."

"You almost sound as if such a crossbred would be superior to our Thoroughbreds."

Ruff shrugged. "In this kind of rough country, I'm sure they would be."

Dixie's expression said clearer than words that she did not agree but saw no point in arguing.

"There's some fine mares in this band," Ruff said, watching Blue Bullet put on a show. The outlaw stallion sensed that High Man and his son, High Fire, were also stallions and that fired his blood. Bugling a challenge, dancing and prancing around his mares, Blue Bullet was a sight to behold.

"We've *got* to save him, Rufus," Dixie said in a wistful voice. "We can't let an animal like that be shot on sight."

"I know," Ruff replied. "But we can't catch what won't be caught and we can no more tame Blue Bullet's wild spirit than we could the free-blowin' wind."

They stayed to watch Blue Bullet's show and study his band of fine mares until daylight grew weak and the first stars appeared. Then Dixie and Ruff reined their horses around and galloped back toward the mouth of the canyon. They tied their stallions to a picket line and made camp for the night, exhausted beyond measure.

Two days later, Johnny Starving Bear opened the canyon's entrance and rode back inside, leading the two Ballou brood mares and his own small family. There was a warm greeting and Johnny seemed pleased with the progress that Ruff and Dixie had made on the wings. He put his wife and children to work helping them pile brush and limbs while he rode out to gather more deadwood. With the new help, Ruff estimated that they would only need one more day before the horse trap was ready to catch Blue Bullet's fine mares. Ruff was glad that the hard footwork was finally almost over.

Watching Johnny Starving Bear riding off in search of another load of deadwood, Dixie said, "That man has a positive genius for knowing how to avoid hard manual labor. But it's obvious he isn't about to allow his wife or little children to become slackers."

"You're just jealous."

"You got that right!"

"Come on," Ruff urged, grabbing a heavy rock and wedging it into the base of an upright pole, "let's get this finished and start having some fun."

"You think separating Blue Bullet from his mares and then driving them into this trap is going to be fun?"

"Yep," Ruff said. "At any rate, it sure will beat the hell out of what we've been doing here up to now."

Dixie had to agree. And the sooner they caught the mares and left this dangerous part of New Mexico Territory, the better.

TWENTY

Dick Hastings stepped down from his sorrel mare and studied fresh tracks. "Four horses. Two of them shod, two others barefoot."

"You reckon it's the Indian and his family?" Ed Rafferty asked.

"Yep, I sure do," Hastings replied. "And since the Indian only owns two horses, I'm wondering who's riding the other pair."

"Could be the Indian was grabbed and forced to go find the boss's mares," another cowboy opinioned.

Hastings nodded. "The tracks are less than a day old and they're leading off toward Blue Bullet's stomping grounds. I reckon we'll just have to follow them and find out."

"Could be the Ballous are riding with the Indian."

"Could be," Hastings said. "Only one way to find out."

Hastings remounted his sorrel and led the four Grimm cowboys off to follow the tracks. Had they been leading in any direction but southwest toward the mustang country, he would not have bothered to follow. But Hastings knew as well as anyone how good a mustanger Johnny Starving Bear was despite his always acting half-crazy. In fact, that was how Johnny had supported his family for many years.

That night, the Grimm Ranch riders made a cold camp and they awoke at dawn under a dark sky that promised a chill rain before noon.

"We'll push hard," Hastings said to his cowboys. "Best

cover as many miles of these tracks as we can before they get washed out."

"Then what'll we do?" a cowboy asked.

"Then we'll just have to look a little harder," Hastings said, thinking the question rather stupid. "Hell, we got eyes, don't we!"

Chastised, the cowboy hurried off to get his saddle. Within five minutes, they were following the Indian's tracks and hearing distant thunder roll across the mountains. Hastings could see pillars of rain clouds feeding down to the north and despite the aching in his old bones, he pushed his mare to her limits. He knew the fastest way to cover a long distance was at a trot. A well-conditioned horse could trot most all day, if it wasn't forced into steep climbs. Trouble was, a trot was a damned uncomfortable gait. You could lean forward and stand in your stirrups for a time, but that exacted a toll on your knees and ankles. Or you could just sort of post like them fancy eastern riders in their fancy flat saddles, but that wasn't much better. Best thing was just to try and sit light in the pants and cushioning the pounding with your legs. Hastings took some comfort in knowing that, while some horses were real spine busters, his sorrel mare was smooth gaited.

The storm held off until late afternoon, and by then Hastings judged that he had cut Johnny's lead in half. The last few hours, they'd climbed into pine country and the horses were gasping in the thinner air.

"Can we take a breather?" a cowboy asked as the rain began to fall, causing the overheated horses to give off clouds of rising steam. "Dick, my horse is starting to get shaky on his feet."

"All right," Hastings said, reining in the mare and feeling a little smug about the fact that he was running younger men and horses into exhaustion while he and the sorrel mare were still capable of setting a blistering pace.

Ed Rafferty was in his forties, ten years younger than Hastings and a good man in the saddle. Even he looked worn down because they'd been riding for almost three days before they'd crossed Starving Bear's tracks.

Ed removed his shapeless hat, turned his face to the rain, and said, "I jest hope that Indian ain't leading his family or the Ballous clear down to Mexico."

Hastings chuckled. "We've been runnin' the dog drop outta ourselves and these horses, but I got a feeling that we'll soon get some decent rest. And when we find the Indian, we'll also find Blue Bullet and those mares."

"You gonna drop him with that big buffalo rifle you brought?" a cowboy asked.

"I reckon, but I won't try and gut-shoot him," Hastings said firmly. "He's as good as dead, though, and even split five ways, a thousand dollars is a fair piece of change."

"Most of a year's wages," another cowboy said. "But I sure don't want to be the one that has to cut off that blue's head so's we can collect the boss's reward."

Hastings frowned without realizing it. So far, he'd been able to avoid thinking about what they'd have to do to the wild stallion once they had him in their rifle sights. His buffalo rifle was really a .52-caliber Sharps breech-loader, ideal for hunting bigger game like grizzly or elk. He had owned the weapon for better than ten years and swore by it even if it still employed the older-style linen-wrapped cartridge, while the newer Henry rifles were all the rage, with their fourteen-shot metallic rim-fire cartridges.

Hastings tightened the oilskin wrapper that covered his Sharps and kept it dry. The rifle would do the job when asked. He could pop the eye out of a gnat at one hundred yards, and—with a little luck and if there was no cross or shifting winds—hit a horse at an honest seven hundred yards.

"Let's get going," Hastings said to his men, "before the tracks are all washed out."

He led the way, pushing the sorrel mare as hard as she could go without risking a fall as the rocks and mud became slippery. Two hours later, the rainsquall was past them and the high country glistened in the warm afternoon sun. A shimmering rainbow straddled forty miles of the prettiest mountain country known to man and reminded him of his childhood fantasy of discovering pots of buried gold at the rainbow's end.

"We got lucky," Rafferty said to no one in particular. "The rain was just a passing cloudburst. Look up yonder along the face of that mountainside. You can still see the tracks pretty clear."

"I've never been in this country before," Hastings called back to his riders. "I thought that Blue Bullet ran about forty miles to the southeast. Maybe this is where he always brought his stolen mares so we'd never find 'em. Keep a sharp eye, boys! I'd like to sneak up on that Indian and try to figure out what he's up to before we jump him."

Late afternoon found them trotting up a wide, low-sided canyon that appeared to be boxed.

"What do you make of this?" Rafferty asked.

"I don't know," Hastings replied. "But you can see as plain as me that there's been a lot of horses up this canyon and they've got to have disappeared someplace."

A half hour later, they were following a narrow trail that bordered a clear stream teeming with fingerling trout. Hastings could feel excitement building inside and when they came to a blocked entrance to what looked like a narrow defile, he knew without saying that they were at the front door of a hidden canyon.

"This must be the place," he said, dismounting and

handing his reins to one of the cowboys.

He yanked his Sharps rifle out of its saddle scabbard. "Ed, come tag along. The rest of you boys just keep still and we'll return shortly."

"I'll bet they're in there," a cowboy said, his voice reflecting their collective anticipation. "I'll bet we not only found that Indian, but also Blue Bullet and the whole damned lot of his mares. Jeezus! The boss is gonna be happy and I'll bet we all get a big bonus in addition to the reward for killing that outlaw stallion."

"Don't spend your money yet," Hastings warned.

He glanced to Ed, who also brought along his rifle. Together, they moved a few branches and burrowed their way through the blockade. Flattening on the ground and staying in the shadows, they stared at the long wings that formed the horse trap.

"You ever see anything like this?" Rafferty whispered.

"Nope. I think we're just a day or two away from a wild horse catching."

"What do you want to do?"

Hastings looked up at the towering canyon walls. "I'd like to swing around and come up on top. We could watch everything from up there and not worry about being seen ourselves."

"Maybe let them do the work and then we step in and reap the rewards?"

"That's the idea," Hastings said. "Though we might just have a fight on our hands when it's our turn to collect."

"There are five of us."

"That's right, and I hope that discourages them from putting up a big fuss."

"And if it doesn't?"

The Grimm Ranch foreman's brow furrowed and he said, "One way or the other, we have our orders and they're to shoot Blue Bullet. If we don't do that, we'd better count ourselves out of work."

"What about the mares?"

Hastings shrugged his shoulders. "I don't think anyone wants bloodshed. Reasonable men usually find reasonable compromises. I don't know the size of Blue Bullet's band of mares, but I'd guess there are quite a few. Enough to satisfy everyone."

Ed Rafferty smiled. "We'll just have to convince the others that compromise is the best answer. Some of our boys are pretty quick to fight."

"I know," Hastings allowed. "But they'll follow my orders or they'll have more fight than they bargained for."

The two men retreated through the blockade and narrow canyon defile. They remounted their horses and the foreman explained what they'd seen and what they were going to do next. He ended by saying, "Any intelligent questions before we backtrail and then find a way up to the rim of the hidden canyon?"

"Well, Dick," a young cowboy named Tony Cassales said, "I just don't understand."

"Don't understand what?"

"Well, I'd as soon just knock that wall of limbs down and ride on into that canyon. Hell, there's five of us and at most three of them. We could probably get the drop on 'em and do whatever we damn well please."

"Tony, that kind of thinking is why you get paid to ride, rope, and shovel corral shit instead of make decisions," Hastings said bluntly.

Tony's cheeks flamed. "Hell, Dick! Why pussyfoot around! We've been riding for the best part of a week. I say we finish up this business and get on back to the ranch."

"Then git!"

"What?"

"Tony, I said git!" Hastings growled. "I won't have a man riding under me that thinks he can think—which you can't. So head on back to the ranch, collect your pay, and don't let me see you again."

"But . . . well, listen! I was just . . ."

Dick Hastings drew his six-gun. He didn't cock back the hammer and he didn't actually point it at Tony, but the message was nonetheless as clear and cold as ice.

"Well, sonofabitch!" Tony wailed. "I've been riding for the outfit almost two years! And now that we're about to make some *real* money, you can't run me off!"

"The hell I can't."

"This is wrong!" Cassales looked to the others, who looked away. His eyes burned with hatred. "God damn the whole lot of you but most especially you, Dick! I won't be forgetting this! And you damned sure ain't seen the last of me!"

"You'd best ride before I shut you up permanently," Hastings warned, his voice beginning to shake with anger.

Cassales cursed, then reined his cow pony around and spurred away.

"Either one of you other boys want to make the decisions?" Hastings asked, excluding his friend Ed Rafferty from the question.

Both cowboys, young but quiet and competent men, shook their heads.

"Good!"

Hastings reined his sorrel mare back down the trail. He felt a twinge of guilt about being so rough on Tony Cassales but there was no room here for an outspoken hothead like that just when things were about to get dicey. A quick-tempered, quick-on-the-trigger fool like young Tony could get people killed with his reckless and independent thinking. Even so, Hastings made a note to make an apology later and perhaps even hire Tony back after the kid cooled down.

Four hours later, they were up on the rim of the canyon, horses tied well back and out of sight or sound.

"It's huge, isn't it!" Rafferty said with wonder as they peered over the lip of the canyon.

"Yep," Hastings agreed, "it's a damn paradise for horses. Big enough to hold maybe fitty year 'round. Probably shel tered from blizzards in winter and there's feed aplenty. I'm surprised that Blue Bullet ever left this canyon."

"He's like some people," Rafferty said. "Greedy."

"Well," Hastings said, "in another day or two, he's going to be dead. I'll put a bullet through his murderin' skull and then we'll face up to the issue of who will own his mares."

"But first we let them catch 'em, right?"

"Right."

Hastings grinned and watched as Ruff, Dixie, and the Indians completed the second wing of the horse trap. "With any luck, it will be ready by tomorrow and they'll have stampeded the stallion and his mares into it the day after. That will give us plenty of time to catch up on our sleep and rest our horses."

"We're all played out, that's for sure."

Dick Hastings watched the work below for another ten minutes before his eyelids began to droop and he yawned. Rolling onto his back and placing his Stetson over his face to shield it from the warm sun, he said, "Wake me up at suppertime."

"Why sure," Ed Rafferty said. "But we're getting pretty low on provisions. Want me to send one of the boys off to hunt if he goes beyond the sound of a rifle shot?"

Hastings lifted his hat and squinted up at his friend. "Just make damn sure that *we* can't hear the sound of the shot.

'Cause if we can hear it, they might, too."

"Sure thing," Rafferty said, easing back from the rim of the canyon.

Dick Hastings replaced his hat back over his eyes. He was smiling. This was going to be fun and profitable. Sure, it was a crying damn shame to kill a horse as magnificent as Blue Bullet, but the big, beautiful bastard was an incurable outlaw. He'd never be ridden again.

One thousand dollars split four ways plus whatever they could get for the captured Thoroughbred mares that they'd claim as belonging to Jack Grimm. It was going to be a fine, fine payday. And the only thing that was yet to be decided was if someone was going to be foolish, greedy, or stubborn enough to get themselves killed.

TWENTY-ONE

"Blue Bullet is getting more nervous every day," Ruff told his sister. "I awoke before dawn this morning and he was less than four hundred yards from our camp. Watching. Our eyes met and he snorted, then turned and raced away."

"He knows that this is the day we will try and steal his mares."

Ruff nursed a cup of steaming coffee. When Johnny Starving Bear had returned with his family, he had also brought everything he owned of value, including coffee, jerky, beans, corn, four halters, two nearly worthless Mexican saddles, three more reatas—two of them broken but neatly spliced back together—a short-handled shovel, and a dull ax, which had still proved enormously useful.

"We're going to run him right into that corral along with his mares. I told Johnny about it yesterday and he got upset."

"Why?"

"He's afraid that Blue Bullet will go crazy and bust out of the canyon through our barricade."

"That's impossible."

"I know," Ruff said, "but failing that, Johnny is worried that the stallion will come storming back up the canyon and hit the gate we're supposed to pull across."

"Now *that*," Dixie said, "*is* entirely possible. But even if the stallion did escape back up the canyon, we could still force him back into the pen a second time."

"It'd be a lot harder," Ruff said. "Right now, Blue Bullet knows that something is afoot but I doubt he has quite figured it out. I'm sure that he still believes that he can escape through those rocks and reach open country. Once he's been trapped, however, he'll know better and it'll be hell to drive him or his mares back into our trap."

"I see what you mean." Dixie sipped and grimaced because Mrs. Starving Bear made the camp coffee so strong. "So what is the alternative?"

"Johnny wants me to shoot the stallion. It's that simple. He argues that, with Blue Bullet out of the picture, everything will be much easier."

"And it's hard to argue that point."

"Exactly." Ruff scowled into his coffee. "I think everyone just wishes that blue outlaw would just disappear."

"He will," Dixie said, "when we pony him up to Colorado or even Wyoming."

"Sure," Ruff said, trying to convince himself that it was really possible.

That morning, they finished the gate that Johnny and his wife were supposed to drag back across the opening wings when the wild horses rushed inside. The gate was nothing more than a rope with brush and branches tied to it. Because it was almost sixty feet long, it had to be light. But they were counting on the fact that Ruff and Dixie, along with the Indians, would quickly lift the rope gate and wave off the predictable backwash of wild horses.

"If Blue Bullet tries to break over the top of us," Johnny said, patting an old holstered Army Colt that now rested on his skinny hips, "I shoot him, by golly!"

Neither Ruff nor Dixie dared argue. If Blue Bullet would not turn back and was intent on trampling them like he'd done Jack Grimm, the only thing that would stop him dead in his tracks would be a well-placed bullet.

By early afternoon, everything was in readiness. Ruff had inspected the entire trap, seeking any opening larger than a man's head and plugging it up with brush so that no horse could possibly view it as an avenue of escape.

"It's solid as we can make it," Ruff announced as he walked back to the opening and jammed his boot into his stirrup. "But we'll only have one easy chance. Let's make it count."

Johnny Starving Bear had already taken his small children up into the rocks and hidden them from view. Now, he and his wife erased their footprints and backtracked to the point of a wing where they'd dug a little pit just big enough to hide themselves. At Ruff's call, they would pop up out of the ground, drag their rope-and-brush "gate" across the opening, and then yell like crazy to scare off Blue Bullet when he discovered that the far end of the trap and canyon was solidly blocked.

Dixie looked at his sister and when they rode back up the canyon, he said, "We'll only have one chance with Blue Bullet, Dixie. If he escapes, we'll either have to let him go or else shoot him. He'll never be driven back down into the trap."

"I know," Dixie said. "Sometimes you seem to forget that I understand horses almost as well as yourself, Ruff."

"Yeah," Ruff said, feeling a little ashamed for stating the obvious. "So let's just do it right the first time."

Up on the rim of the canyon, Dick Hastings and his three men tensed with anticipation.

Dick said, "They're rolling the dice and unless I miss my bet, they're going to come up snake eyes."

"What do you mean?" Ed Rafferty asked.

"I mean that Blue Bullet won't allow himself to be caught in that brush trap. He'll shoot through it like grain through a goose. And look out if either one of those Ballous are in his way 'cause he'll stampede right over the top of them."

"And when that happens?"

Hastings eased his Spencer rifle up to the lip of the canyon. "If I get a clean shot, I'll settle the issue once and for all."

"Be a hell of a shot," one of the cowboys said. "Might be we should all join in."

Hastings considered that and then he nodded his head in agreement. Each of his men had brought rifles, expecting to be the one that dropped Blue Bullet. And while the Grimm Ranch foreman did not know how many marksman he had riding with him, it certainly could not hurt to have some backup.

"All right," he said, "but if that stallion escapes, I'll take the first shot. If Blue Bullet stays on his feet, he's open game. He'll have to come flying up-canyon right past our rifle sights. I figure even shooting down at an angle, one of us ought to be able to drop him. And once he's down, we can take our time and put the murdering, mare-stealin' sonofabitch out of his misery."

The cowboys went to retrieve their rifles, except for Rafferty, who hesitated. "Are you so sure that he will break out of that horse trap?"

"Yep," Hastings said without hesitation. "And if he don't, then we'll just back off the ridge, ride around to the entrance, and shoot him at close range."

"We do that, the Ballous are going to go plumb crazy."

"Can't be helped," Hastings said heavily. "We got our orders. I'm getting old and you're no spring chicken, Ed. We need that reward money on the stallion's head. Savvy?"

"I'm afraid I do," Ed Rafferty answered, "but I sure hate to kill that blue stallion. To me, he's a damn near a work of art and a sure enough New Mexico legend."

"Legend?" Hastings repeated, checking his rifle as he weighed the word in his mind. "That may be true, Ed, but legends are generally things from the past. That's what we're going to make Blue Bullet—a thing of the past."

If it was meant to be a joke, Rafferty didn't laugh. Instead, he went to get his own rifle, also a Sharps but of an older, lighter-caliber vintage. It wasn't nearly the equal to Dick Hastings's heavier weapon, but he'd shot a hell of a lot of game with it over the years and it was plenty capable of bringing down a horse.

"Here we go," Hastings said a few minutes later as they watched Ruff and Dixie push their Thoroughbred stallions into a gallop and fan out to follow the sides of the canyon. "They're going to flank, then drive them right down past us."

"Maybe we should shoot the stallion now," one of the cowboys offered.

"No!" Hastings lowered his voice. "For the last time, if Blue Bullet breaks back and comes flying up the canyon alone, we open fire. If he stays trapped, we go down and shoot him at close range. Is that understood?"

"Yes, sir," the cowboys echoed, probably remembering how Tony had been fired for voicing his strong and angry objections.

With that settled, Dick Hastings laid his cheek on his rifle and prepared to watch the show.

"Hee-yaw!" Ruff shouted, driving High Fire hard up the canyon floor and then slicing in toward the rear of the wild horses just as Dixie was closing in from the opposite side.

Blue Bullet bugled his angry challenge and, for a moment, Ruff actually thought that the stallion was going to charge and try to topple him and his Thoroughbred in a furious charge with ears laid back and yellow teeth bared. But at the very last instant, Blue Bullet wavered and decided to drive his mares down the valley.

"We got 'em on the run!" Dixie shouted over the thunder of hoofbeats.

Ruff pushed High Fire hard and yet did not crowd the wild horse herd as it streamed down the canyon with Blue Bullet nipping at the tails of his mares.

"Give him some room!" Ruff shouted as Blue Bullet actually whirled to charge Dixie atop old High Man.

Dixie reined her horse off and let the blue stallion chase her for about fifty yards, closing the gap with every powerful stride. Dixie and High Man would have been in deep trouble if Blue Bullet hadn't felt compelled to stop, spin, and race after his fleeing mares.

"Stay back until we get near the catch pen, then crowd them hard!" Ruff shouted, doubting that his words could even be heard by Dixie amid all the pounding hoofbeats.

For a moment, Ruff held his breath as the lead mare of the band snorted, shied, and acted as if she might swerve away from the spooky-looking wings. But there were so many horses racing in her wake that the mare would have been knocked over and trampled had she tried to stop. With little choice but to keep running, she shot in between the outstretched wings and was followed by the entire band with Blue Bullet closing in on the rear.

The moment they were inside, Ruff saw Johnny Starving Bear and his wife leap from their hiding places and sprint across the opening, dragging the heavy rope covered with brush to make it seem a more formidable gate. Ruff and Dixie reined up hard and their stallions skidded to a halt even as Blue Bullet bolted back through the herd, realizing that he was snared.

"Yaaaaa!" Ruff shouted, hearing Dixie and the Indians screaming at the top of their lungs.

But Blue Bullet was determined not to be trapped. Ignoring the flimsy rope-and-brush barrier, he dashed straight at Johnny Starving Bear with his ears laid back tight and eyes filled with demons. The Indian dropped the rope and clawed for his pistol but he was too late. Blue Bullet struck him running and the impact catapulted Johnny up into the air. His wife cried as if she herself had been trampled. She dropped the rope gate as the outlaw stallion swept past and ran to her husband, who lay writing in agony.

Ruff grabbed up the rope and leaned into it with all of his strength as Blue Bullet's mares tried to follow their leader. Dixie drove High Man at the charging mares, firing her Navy Colt and screaming at the top of her lungs. The lead mare, a fine bay Thoroughbred, shied away, and the others followed her around and around in the huge trap.

"Keep riding up and down the line!" Ruff yelled to his sister as he leaned back and threw all his weight against the rope, trying to keep it from sagging to the ground. "Keep firing that gun! Here, use my revolver!"

Dixie did keep firing and somehow, the mares were contained. Falling back, eyes rolling with fear, they circled inside the trap like fish in a bowl.

"Dixie! Come over here!" Ruff yelled. "Let's wrap this rope around your saddle horn and pull it across and tie it to the other wing! We've got to keep it up or those mares will come back through."

Dixie took the rope and did as Ruff ordered. It took only seconds to get to the other wing to a spot where Ruff managed to tie it securely. It had all happened so fast that he hadn't time to watch Blue Bullet streak back up the canyon for freedom. And when he did, he realized that all the thunder filling his ears was not from hoofbeats alone.

"Rifle fire!" he yelled. "They're . . . they're trying to kill Blue Bullet!"

Dixie followed Ruff's gaze and also saw the puffs of smoke that marked the hiding place of the shooters. And even as she watched, she saw Blue Bullet stagger, fall, and then struggle to rise again.

"They're killing him!"

Ruff watched helplessly as four rifles boomed repeatedly, their shots blanketing the canyon. Blue Bullet regained his feet and raced on toward the high end of the box canyon but it didn't take a horseman to see that he had been hit and was faltering as he vanished into the cover of distant rocks and trees.

Ruff knew that he was helpless to save Blue Bullet from the marksmen above. So he did the only thing he could, and that was to hurry over to Johnny Starving Bear's side, where his wife and little children were gathered.

"How is he?" Ruff asked, stupidly forgetting that the Indians didn't understand English.

"Hey, white face," Johnny gritted, opening his eyes. "Did you shoot that crazy stud horse for us? I need the money."

"No," Ruff said. "Someone else did."

Johnny's eyes widened in alarm and he gripped Ruff's wrist. "That money belongs to us!"

"The stallion is still on its feet."

"Then *you* shoot it!"

"I can't. Besides, we captured all his mares! They're worth . . ."

Before Ruff could finish, Johnny was pushing himself up to a sitting position. His wife helped him to his feet.

"You shouldn't move yet," Ruff warned. "You don't know what is broken. You should stay down, Johnny!"

But the Indian wasn't listening. Bent over in pain, he found his pistol, threw off his wife's clutching hands, and limped over to where they had hidden their saddle horses.

A few moments later, the Indian emerged from the trees on horseback and kicked his mount into a trot, heading up the canyon.

"Ruff?" Dixie asked. "Ruff, he's either going to get killed by that stallion or he'll shoot him!"

"I know."

"We have to stop him!"

Ruff started to climb back on High Fire but the Indian woman cried out in rage. She pulled a knife from under her dress and shrieked, forcing Ruff while making it clear that he was not to interfere with her badly injured husband.

"Then I'll go!" Dixie cried.

"No!"

Dixie froze. Her head swiveled back and forth, from Ruff to up-canyon, where Johnny was riding bent over in pain. A plaintive question filled her throat. "Ruff?"

"It's done," he heard himself tell her. "If Johnny doesn't kill Blue Bullet, then those men up on top will finish the job. His outlaw days are over. He's got nowhere else to run."

"Oh yeah? Look!" Dixie suddenly cried, jumping up and down with excitement and pointing up the canyon.

Ruff's eyes jerked past his sister to see the blue stallion laboring up the side of the canyon wall. Up what he and Dixie had both considered a "goat trail." And not only was Blue Bullet navigating the impossibly steep and narrow path, but he was doing it in a hurry.

"The riflemen can't see him from on top," Ruff said to himself. "Those men up on top can't see him until he crests the rim!"

They all held their breath as the stallion traversed the harrowing switchbacks. Once his feet slipped and Dixie gasped. But somehow, the blue stallion managed to regain his footing and then he was humping over the rim. He paused at the rim for an instant moment to call one last time for his lost mares.

They all heard Blue Bullet's final bugling farewell. It floated down the canyon like a strong winter's wind and echoed between the high rock walls. It ended with the sound of a rifle shot as Blue Bullet wheeled and raced away. Ruff thought that his mind might have been playing tricks and he was imagining everything. But the rifle shot washed over him, struck the canyon's mouth, then flowed back again, and Ruff knew in the marrow of his bones that Blue Bullet had escaped one more time. Maybe to die of his wounds, but at least to die free.

"Let's get these mares settled down," he said as Johnny Starving Bear appeared, still bent over his horse's withers. "And then let's see if we can help Johnny."

"I'm glad he wasn't able to shoot that blue stallion," Dixie whispered, her voice cracked with emotion.

Ruff watched the Indian woman and her children stream up the canyon to help Johnny. He hoped that the Indian would recover, and suspected that, in time, he would. And as for the men up on top, well, the mares were now captured and claimed.

"What's going to happen when those men come?" Dixie asked.

"Depends on them," Ruff told his sister. "Johnny is out two horses and he almost got himself killed a few minutes ago. We won't give away what we earned. But don't worry. I recognized Dick Hastings and you said he's a good and reasonable man."

"Oh, he is!" Dixie smiled with relief. "He might hate that stallion, but he won't dare try and steal these mares."

"I'm real glad to hear that."

Dixie was quiet a long time, just watching the mares settle. Finally, she asked what was on both their minds.

"Ruff, do you think he got away?"

"Yes, Dixie, I do."

"And . . . and do you think he'll live?"

"Sure he will," Ruff said, gently mussing Dixie's hair and grinning down at her pretty but worried face. " 'Cause we both know that legends never die."

Dixie must have liked that answer because she brightened, then hurried off to see what she could do to help Johnny Starving Bear.

TWENTY-TWO

When Dick Hastings and his three men arrived back down at the mouth of the canyon, they dismounted and tied their horses. Peering through the barricade at Blue Bullet's captured mares, they could identify at least half of them that had once belonged to Jack Grimm.

"What are we going to do?" Ed Rafferty asked. "That damned outlaw stallion is probably still running. We'll never catch him now."

"True enough," Hastings said. "I thought sure he was planted, but maybe legends never die. I don't know about that. What I do know is that we're taking these mares, or at least a fair number of 'em. I'm hoping they'll buy us our jobs."

"I sure as hell hope so," Rafferty said. "It ought to work. Some of these mares were born in England and France. You know that better than I do, Dick. Some of 'em cost Jack thousands of dollars."

"*All* of them did," Hastings corrected.

"So how are we going to handle this?" one of the young cowboys asked nervously.

Hastings frowned. This was a tough one. There wasn't any doubt that, in order to save their jobs, they could not come back empty-handed. On the other hand, the Ballous and Johnny Starving Bear had a legitimate claim on the mares because they'd been the ones to finally catch them.

"Let's let the dust settle and give it a little time," Hastings decided. "Come evening, we'll skinny on through this

193

barricade, circle around the mares and have a powwow with Rufus Ballou and his sister."

"If we had a bottle of whiskey, we could buy off Johnny Starving Bear cheap," a cowboy said, trying to lighten the mood.

"I doubt that," Hastings said in a curt voice. "Johnny may not crazy, but he's not. I saw through his game years ago, And he'll fight if he's cornered."

"Then we shouldn't corner him," Rafferty said.

"That's right," Hastings allowed. "We'll just play it firm, but not too tough. I'm willing to divvy up those mares."

"Yeah," Rafferty said, "but are they?"

It was dusk when the mares started to suddenly get excited again and then Hastings and another man that Dixie recognized appeared.

"Hello, Miss Ballou," Hastings said, removing his hat. "I congratulate all of you for catching Mr. Grimm's mares for him."

"They're wild and unclaimed as far as we're concerned," Dixie said in a cold voice. "And I'll never forgive you for trying to shoot down Blue Bullet from up on the rim of the canyon."

"We were just doing our job," Hastings said, noticing that Johnny Starving Bear was packing a pistol.

"You'll get none of these mares," Ruff said. "As for Blue Bullet, well, I don't know if you did your job or not, but—"

"We didn't," Hastings snapped. "The stallion was definitely hit, we saw drops of blood but it didn't appear to be a kill shot and he's gone. Probably halfway to Arizona or Colorado by now."

"Good!"

"But the mares do belong to Mr. Grimm and we mean

to take them back."

"Over our dead bodies," Ruff said.

"I got a whole bunch of men camped just outside this canyon," Hastings bluffed.

"You got two, maybe three," Ruff corrected. "If you'd have had more, they'd have been firing down at Blue Bullet along with all the rest of you sharpshooting horse killers."

Hastings blushed with anger. "Maybe we should talk a deal."

"No deal."

Hastings drew a long, ragged breath and he suddenly looked old. Turning to Dixie, he said, "You know I'm a fair man, Miss Ballou. And I treated you well when you were at the ranch."

"That's true."

"Then talk to your brother. Make him see that we can't go back without something for Mr. Grimm or we'll lose our jobs."

Dixie sighed. She turned to her brother. "He *will* be fired and so will the rest of them. And if we don't strike a deal, I'm afraid that Jack will never let up on us. He'll hound us wherever we go."

Ruff looked to Johnny Starving Bear. "We're equal partners. What do you say?"

"Give 'em the three back that stallion took last week, plus let them pick three more," Johnny said. "We keep the rest."

"That ain't enough!" Hastings protested.

"I'm afraid that it will just have to be," Ruff said. "Six blooded Thoroughbred mares ought to ease Jack Grimm's pain. That's the deal. Take it or leave it."

Hastings glanced sideways to his friend. "Ed, what do you think? Should we put up a fight?"

"You mean now?"

"Two against two," Hastings said. "Miss Ballou is out of this."

"Not by a long shot, I'm not!"

"Then dammit," Hastings growled, "we'll accept your paltry offer rather than shed blood."

Ruff shifted his hand away from his gun. "I'm glad that you are the reasonable man that Dixie described. Pick your three extra mares."

"You're a hard man to deal with," Hastings said. "We'll go back to our camp and do the splitting off tomorrow at first light."

"That'd be fine," Ruff said, feeling good about the compromise. Of the remaining two dozen or so mares, he and Dixie would get sixteen, and almost all of them would be top-quality imported Thoroughbreds. They'd sell off enough to buy the horse ranch of their dreams and keep the very best for their own breeding program.

In the morning, true to his word, Dick Hastings brought his men into the catch pen and sorted out the mares that he was to return to his boss. At the same time, Ruff, Dixie, and Johnny chose their own horses and began to rope and collect them with makeshift halters.

"This is almost like suddenly getting our entire horse ranch back," Dixie said, barely able to contain her pleasure and excitement. "It would all be perfect if we had Blue Bullet back."

"No," Ruff corrected, "it wouldn't be perfect if that stallion was to reappear. It would be chaos. Believe me, Dixie, this is for the best."

Dixie had to agree. And that afternoon, when they had all the Thoroughbred mares haltered and gentled down a little, they removed the barricade.

"Well," Hastings said, hanging back with Ed Rafferty as

his two younger cowboys led their mares out of the canyon, "I have to tell you that you'd best keep riding and never come back to Rum River."

"That makes sense," Ruff said. "And . . ."

"Hold it!"

Ruff looked up suddenly to see a man up in the rocks with a six-gun clenched in his fist.

"Tony!" Hastings shouted. "What the hell!"

"I'm going to take all the mares back to Mr. Grimm! And I'll tell him just what happened out here. How you let Blue Bullet get away and then *gave away* all but a handful of his mares."

"Tony, put down that pistol before someone gets shot!"

"No." The young man grinned coldly. "Dick, you thought that you could run me off and cheat Mr. Grimm out of his mares by giving in to these people. But I won't let that happen!"

Dick Hastings rolled his eyes at Ruff to indicate that he was to step away. Ruff retreated a few halting steps and, out of the corner of his eye, he saw Johnny Starving Bear and Dixie do the same.

"Now, Tony," Hastings was saying, "maybe I was a little rough when I sent you packing, but—"

"Shut up!" Tony cried. "By the time this is over, *I'll* have your damn job and a bonus from Mr. Grimm that'll choke a mule!"

The ranch foreman managed a thin smile. "Hell, Tony, you can have my job if you want. Take it! I quit. Ed, you quit, too, don't you?"

"Why, sure," Ed Rafferty blurted. "I don't need no ranch job anymore. I've been getting itchy footed lately."

"You're both *liars*!"

Hastings swallowed and was about to say something when one of the other cowboys, a kid that didn't look more than twenty jumped back through the narrow canyon's entrance with a gun in his fist and a scared but determined look on his face.

"No!" Hastings shouted, clawing for his own pistol just as Ruff's hand struck the butt of his Colt.

Tony Cassales wounded the kid and tried to turn his gun back on the ranch foreman but never had a chance. Ruff's Army Colt led a volley of bullets that knocked Tony crashing into the stream that bled through the horse canyon.

"Are you hit bad!" Hastings shouted, jumping to the aid of his young cowboy.

"No, just winged," the cowboy gritted, holstering his gun.

"In that case," Hastings said, smashing the kid with his fist and flattening him to the ground, "you deserve to have your teeth knocked down your throat for almost getting me shot!"

The young man was bleeding from a bullet's nick across his ribs and a rapidly swelling lower lip. "Kee-rist!" he muttered. "You firin' me, too, Mr. Hastings?"

Hastings looked at Dixie. "Miss Ballou, this young fella did a real foolish thing. Do you think he deserves to keep his job?"

"I do," Dixie said without hesitation as she went to attend the young cowboy's wounds. "And since you'll probably get to keep *your* job, and since Blue Bullet will never return to this country, I think you should show some mercy and even gratitude."

"She's right," offered a shaken-looking Ed Rafferty. "Besides, he's a top hand. And furthermore, you swore him and the rest of us to secrecy about missing that blue outlaw when it raced across the path of your rifle sights."

Hastings scrubbed his jaw and finally nodded. "All right," he said, starting for his horse. "But if the boss gives me hell about letting Blue Bullet get away, then he buys the whiskey and I pick the line camp we hole up in while Mr. Grimm cools down. Agreed?"

The wounded cowboy, eyes full of pain and Dixie, nodded with a loose smile, and that was when they all heard Blue Bullet's bugling challenge from atop the canyon's high rim.

"Well, I'll be damned," Ruff said with a wide grin. "The legend has already returned!"

Ed Hastings paled and his jaw dropped. Dixie beamed while Johnny Starving Bear threw his head to the sky and giggled like crazy.

If you enjoyed this book, subscribe now and get...

TWO FREE

A $7.00 VALUE–

If you would like to read more of the very best, most exciting, adventurous, action-packed Westerns being published today, you'll want to subscribe to True Value's Western Home Subscription Service.

Each month the editors of True Value will select the 6 very best Westerns from America's leading publishers for special readers like you. You'll be able to preview these new titles as soon as they are published, *FREE* for ten days with no obligation!

TWO FREE BOOKS

When you subscribe, we'll send you your first month's shipment of the newest and best 6 Westerns for you to preview. With your first shipment, two of these books will be yours as our introductory gift to you absolutely *FREE* (a $7.00 value), regardless of what you decide to do. If

you like them, as much as we think you will, keep all six books but pay for just 4 at the low subscriber rate of just $2.75 each. If you decide to return them, keep 2 of the titles as our gift. No obligation.

Special Subscriber Savings

When you become a True Value subscriber you'll save money several ways. First, all regular monthly selections will be billed at the low subscriber price of just $2.75 each. That's at least a savings of $4.50 each month below the publishers price. Second, there is never any shipping, handling or other hidden charges—*Free home delivery*. What's more there is no minimum number of books you must buy, you may return any selection for full credit and you can cancel your subscription at any time. A TRUE VALUE!

A special offer for people who enjoy reading the best Westerns published today.

WESTERNS!

NO OBLIGATION

Mail the coupon below

To start your subscription and receive 2 FREE WESTERNS, fill out the coupon below and mail it today. We'll send your first shipment which includes 2 FREE BOOKS as soon as we receive it.

Mail To: **True Value Home Subscription Services, Inc. P.O. Box 5235**
120 Brighton Road, Clifton, New Jersey 07015-5235

YES! I want to start reviewing the very best Westerns being published today. Send me my first shipment of 6 Westerns for me to preview FREE for 10 days. If I decide to keep them. I'll pay for just 4 of the books at the low subscriber price of $2.75 each; a total $11.00 (a $21.00 value). Then each month I'll receive the 6 newest and best Westerns to preview Free for 10 days. If I'm not satisfied I may return them within 10 days and owe nothing. Otherwise I'll be billed at the special low subscriber rate of $2.75 each; a total of $16.50 (at least a $21.00 value) and save $4.50 off the publishers price. There are never any shipping. handling or other hidden charges. I understand I am under no obligation to purchase any number of books and I can cancel my subscription at any time. no questions asked. In any case the 2 FREE books are mine to keep.

Name _____

Street Address _____ Apt. No. _____

City _____ State _____ Zip Code _____

Telephone _____

Signature _____
(if under 18 parent or guardian must sign)

Terms and prices subject to change. Orders subject
to acceptance by True Value Home Subscription
Services. Inc.

944-7